The Runaway Bus Mystery

A Case Book Mystery

The Runaway Bus Mystery

by Irwin Touster
and Richard Curtis

pictures by Richard Cuffari

The Dial Press : New York

Library of Congress Cataloging in Publication Data
Touster, Irwin, 1921–
The runaway bus mystery. (The Case book mystery series)
Summary: With the help of a lawyer friend, three children
investigate a controversial bus accident.
[1. Mystery stories] I. Curtis, Richard, joint author.
II. Cuffari, Richard, 1925– illus. III. Title.
PZ7.T6483Ru [Fic] 72–713

With love to Josh and David

Contents

The Runaway Bus Mystery

1
Crash!

Merton Pringle didn't usually look at his feet when he walked. He liked to stride as if he were fifty years younger, marching again in World War I, head high, arms swinging freely, legs propelling him with springy ease. But he had just left his daughter's home after spending the day with his three grandchildren, and he was deeply absorbed in thought.

Thus when he arrived at the corner of Mason Street and Temple Avenue, his eyes were lowered. He glanced up just long enough to make sure the traffic light was green, then started to cross. He had taken three steps when he heard the blare of a horn to his left. He looked in that direction and saw a sunflower-yellow school bus speeding down the steep curving slope of the avenue that brought traffic from the west into the town of Aubrey Park.

Anger welled up in Pringle's throat. "That bus is going much too fast," he said to himself, jumping back to the safety of the sidewalk. With the impression of his laughing grandchildren still fresh in his mind, he was appalled that a driver should take such risks with the lives of young people.

When the bus swerved into the opposite lane to avoid a slow-moving car in front of it, Pringle's anger turned to horror. "That driver must be a maniac!" he exclaimed. Luckily, no car had been in the other lane, but now as the bus returned to its proper side of the street Pringle saw that it wasn't slowing down for the red light. A mother halfway across Temple snatched up her two children and staggered the rest of the way, tripping over the curb and sprawling onto the sidewalk. The bus, still beeping madly, was now close enough for him to see the driver's face, a pink, grizzled face that flashed teeth as if the man was laughing. "He's drunk!" Pringle cried as the bus streaked past him.

Ahead of the bus now a gardener's truck cruised toward town, its rear sagging under the weight of three trees destined for some suburban backyard. The bus bore down on it, going at least twice the legal speed limit of twenty-five miles an hour. A gardener sitting with the trees jumped to his feet and waved his arms at the bus. When he saw it was useless, he bailed out, dropping over the side of the truck. His momentum carried him twenty windmill steps before he tripped and flew headfirst into a thick hedge.

At the last moment the bus tried to swerve away from the truck but clipped a corner of it. Bus and truck catapulted over a curb and slammed into the brick side wall of a supermarket, ramming a long train of shopping carts and sending

them careening crazily into the parking lot. There was a sickening clanging and crunching of metal as the two vehicles bounced off the wall and the shopping carts highballed into an ice machine.

As fast as his aging legs could carry him, Pringle trotted to the supermarket. Neither of the vehicles had overturned, but the right sides of both were crumpled as if a giant boot had kicked them. Two of the trees had bounced out of the truck and were now thrusting branches up around the windshield of the bus, making it look like a bizarre greenhouse. Although no more than ten seconds had elapsed since the accident, the supermarket had emptied and a rapidly swelling throng was milling around the vehicles.

"Call the police!" someone was shouting. "Call the fire department!" "Call an ambulance!" "Get the kids out of there before fire breaks out!" shouted others.

Pringle came to the hedge that the gardener had flown into and helped the poor fellow out. If the matter hadn't been so serious it would have been comical. His old floppy hat had been shoved down so hard over his ears that the brim was half torn off. Twigs and leaves adhered to his lips, nose, and overalls, and he was hurling rapid-fire oaths at the school bus in a language Pringle didn't understand.

They hastened to the wreckage. Already, in the background, the sound of approaching sirens pierced the air. But it was another sound that Pringle cocked his ear for: the cries of injured children. And when he realized he didn't hear them, his heart sank, for it meant that the children might be more than injured.

But he was wrong on that score. A young man with shoulder-length blond hair and a headband had managed to climb through the foliage blocking the door and force his way into the bus. "I don't see any kids here," he shouted to the anxious crowd, who let out a collective sigh of relief. "Just the driver. Where are the police?"

At that very moment a police car pulled up, followed by two more, two ambulances, and a fire truck. The men jumped out of their vehicles before they'd even come to a halt, leaving the doors open and motors running. Hoses were unrolled, stretchers brought up, and the crowd pressed back to a safe distance in case the gasoline spilled in the collision should ignite. Cars continued arriving as members of the volunteer fire department came from every direction.

The branches blocking the bus door were quickly chopped away. Medical workers went in and moments later carried out a stretcher bearing the driver. His face was bloody but he was obviously alive, squirming and groaning. The workers hustled him into one of the ambulances, which pulled out like a dragster, spinning rubber in a race with death.

"Did anyone witness this accident?" a policeman was yelling to the crowd at large. "Is there anyone here who saw what happened?"

"I did," Pringle replied, pushing his way through.

The policeman, a tall rugged-faced man, looked at him skeptically. "Are you sure you actually saw it?" he said to the old man. "Everybody was here moments after it happened, but I want someone who witnessed it as it was occurring."

"Yes," Pringle assured him. "I saw the whole thing." The policeman summoned a man in a business suit and introduced him as a detective. They both had pads and pens poised to record Pringle's story, and several dozen bystanders formed a circle around them to hear it.

"I was crossing the street when I heard the bus beeping. I looked up and this drunken maniac was coming down the hill at a hundred miles an hour—"

"Just a moment," the detective interrupted him. "It's vital that the information we collect here be accurate, Mr. Pringle. So we're going to have to ask you to state only what you actually observed. If you can't support your observations they'll be of no value to us. You've called the driver a drunken maniac and said he was coming down the hill at a hundred miles an hour. How do you know these things? Was he waving a liquor bottle as he went by? How could you measure his speed? These are the kind of facts we're seeking."

Pringle tried to comply with their request for a calm, objective, accurate report, but he was too upset. His mind kept flashing images of what might have happened had the bus been loaded with children. He interjected remarks like "How they could license a drunken bum like that is a mystery," and "That nut must have had the gas pedal all the way to the floor."

Among the shoppers inside the Better Brands Supermarket was Mrs. Virginia Parsons. She had been standing near the north wall removing a coffee can from the top of a pyramid when the wall seemed to jump at her with an explosive sound, showering her with cans. She fell to the floor and lay dazed for a minute, wondering if there had been an earthquake. Then she tried to get up, but every time she did she stepped on a can and fell again, looking like a skater venturing onto ice for the first time.

She finally managed to get to her feet, picked her shopping bag off the floor, tested her body for bruises, and, finding none, made for the cash registers. By that time almost everyone had evacuated the store.

When she stepped outside her hand flew to her mouth. "My son! Raymond! Raymond!" she cried, running to the bus. A young man with long hair seized her arm. "It's all right. There were no children in there," he told her. "The bus must have been on the way back to the garage after dropping the last child off." He pointed to his watch. It was a little after four.

She waited with the rest of the curious spectators for the police to come. Within moments it seemed as if every uniformed person in the town had descended on the scene, and she watched as the injured driver was placed in the ambulance. Although his face was bloody, she recognized Sam Gilman. She bit her lip. Sam had been driving children to school for as long as anyone in the community could remember, and they all adored him. She herself didn't care for Sam all that much because of certain things she had heard about him from some of the other parents—such as his tendency to let the kids horse around on the bus instead of keeping strict discipline. That sort of thing, she had told members of the Parent-Teacher Association, of which she was vice-president, could lead to an accident if Sam let his attention be distracted. She didn't like anyone who didn't take life as seriously as she did. Still, she felt sorry to see him hurt this way.

She wandered over to a small knot of people standing around a policeman, a man in a business suit, and an old man. She craned her neck and saw the old man gesticulating wildly as the other two calmly wrote down what he said. She heard only snatches of his testimony, such as "drunk" and "laughing like a maniac" and "That nut must have had the gas pedal all the way to the floor."

"Is he talking about the driver of the gardener's truck?" she asked a woman on the fringe of the crowd.

"No, the bus driver."

Mrs. Parsons frowned. "The bus driver!"

"Yes," the woman said. "The old man says he saw the whole thing. The bus driver was drunk and drove at about a hundred miles an hour through the red light and into the truck, and they both crashed into the wall. Can you imagine? What kind of people do they hire these days?"

Mrs. Parsons' sympathy for Sam evaporated in a flash. "I always said something like this would happen," she muttered. "Someone's head will roll if I have anything to say about it."

She picked up her groceries and was about to get into her car when she heard shouts. People were running toward the school bus. She put her groceries down and ran with them. A policeman was standing in the door of the bus, yelling at two white-clad men standing by an ambulance. "Don't leave! There's a kid in here. I just found him at the back of the bus."

The medical workers grabbed a stretcher and came running as the police formed a cordon and pushed the gawking spectators back. Several mothers cried their children's names, and Mrs. Parsons' heart beat wildly as she wondered if the lone victim in the bus was her own son. A tense minute passed until the men emerged with a stretcher. The boy on it, unconscious, a thin stream of blood trickling from his left temple, was too old to be Raymond, but she thought it looked like someone she knew. "Who is it?" several people asked.

The policeman who had discovered the boy was carrying three ring-binder notebooks. He opened one, running his finger through several pages, searching for a name. Then he looked up and said, "Does anyone here know a Vernon Stevenson?"

2

A Sleepless Night

Even at the best of times, breakfasts in the Case household were not particularly talkative. Mr. Case liked to read his newspaper in peace, Mrs. Case was busy running back and forth between kitchen and dining room, and Penny and David usually had their noses buried in school books. The family saved important communications for dinner, when there was time to go into them at length.

This morning the breakfast table was as silent as a funeral. In fact, thoughts of real funerals were preying on each of their minds. They had heard news of the accident the night before and received half a dozen phone calls from people who knew that Vernon Stevenson was David and Penny's closest friend. They had heard varying descriptions of Vernon's condition when pulled from the bus, but all their efforts to reach Vernon's parents to learn how serious his injury was had been fruitless. All they got was the one-word description "serious" when they spoke to a nurse on the phone. That was an official classification, and the only consoling thing about it was that it was less grave than "critical." Still, "serious" covered a multitude of injuries; one could be horribly maimed yet not be on the critical list. Or some delayed symptom, such as internal bleeding, could turn a serious injury into a critical or maybe even a fatal one.

No one in the Case family had slept very much that night. They barely touched their breakfasts. Mr. Case had just stood up and said, "I think I'll try the Stevensons again" when the phone rang. The four rushed into the den but Mr. Case got there first. "Martha? We've been trying to get you since last night. Yes, of course you were. You must be exhausted. How's Vernon?" Mrs. Case and David and Penny crowded around Mr. Case. "Mmm. Mmm. Mmm," he said, nodding. In reply to their questioning looks he held up his hand to indicate Vernon was going to be all right. "What about Sam Gilman?" he asked. "Mmm. How did it happen?"

There was a long silence and Penny and David strained to hear what Vernon's mother was saying. Mr. Case began to frown. "Are they sure? That doesn't sound like Sam. Yes. Yes, I see. I suppose we won't know until they let us speak to Sam. But tell me this: what was Vernon doing on the bus if it was heading back to the garage?" The Cases leaned forward eagerly. For the first time Mr. Case smiled. "That does sound like Vernon. Is there anything we can do? Of course we will. David and Penny will go over there today. Now, don't worry about a thing, Martha. It sounds like he's in good hands at the hospital."

The second he hung up Penny and David spewed out questions like machine-gun bullets. "How is he?" "What was he doing in the bus?" "What actually happened?" "How's Sam?"

Their father held up his palms, returned to the dining room, and drank some coffee. "Ah, now I feel human again," he said. His family sat down around him. "Vernon's got a broken leg and a mild concussion, but the doctors, including his father, don't believe there's been any brain damage."

"Thank heavens," Mrs. Case said. "If anything happened to that fine mind of his it would be tragic."

"Fine mind indeed," said Mr. Case. "It's his fine mind that got him in the hospital."

"What does that mean?" Penny asked with a touch of indignation. She was very fond of Vernon and didn't like any suggestion that he could do something stupid.

"Apparently he was so engrossed diagramming one of those scientific experiments he's always dreaming up that he didn't hear Sam call out his stop. He was slumped down in the back of the bus using the seat next to him as a drafting board, so Sam had no idea there was a passenger left on the bus. Sam, by the way, also has a concussion, plus bruises and a broken arm. They're both at Aubrey Park General Hospital. You'll be able to see them this afternoon after school. Visiting hours are four to six in the afternoon, seven to nine in the evening."

"How did it happen?" Penny asked.

"And what did you mean when you said, 'That doesn't sound like Sam'?" David added.

"Well," said Mr. Case, "there are conflicting reports and nobody will know for sure until Sam is allowed to have visitors. But from what Mrs. Stevenson told me, Sam seems to have been driving recklessly."

"Recklessly?" Penny gasped. "Sam?"

"You heard me say it didn't sound like him. But they have a witness who claims Sam was speeding coming down the hill on Temple and went through a red light. Almost ran over a woman and two children. He rammed a truck and they both crashed into the Better Brands Supermarket. Luckily, no one else was hurt."

The children looked dazed. "Sam?" Penny murmured again, shaking her head as if the idea wouldn't fall into the right slot in her brain.

"There is some suggestion Sam was drinking," Mr. Case added gravely.

David's head snapped back as if he'd been punched. "Sam drinking? Never! I've been Sam's passenger since nursery school. He hasn't had so much as a sip of orange pop on the job."

"He may have been drinking before he boarded the bus," Mrs. Case pointed out.

"I'm telling you, Mom, Sam wouldn't do that. He told me so once when I was kidding around with him. He waved his hands at me and said, 'I'd cut these off before risking the lives of my passengers.' "

"That's right," Penny chimed in. "He says we're like his own children."

"There may have been special circumstances," Mr. Case said.

"What does that mean?" Penny asked.

"I mean, he may have been under unusual emotional pressure. A quarrel at home or some other worry."

"I refuse to believe it," David insisted.

"There'll be an inquiry," Mr. Case said calmly, "and then we'll get to the truth. Let's try to finish our breakfast."

They stared glumly at their plates.

"I guess I'll just have something at the office," Mr. Case said, getting slowly to his feet.

"We'll grab a bite at school," David said.

The phone rang and everyone jumped. Penny dashed into the den. "It's for you, Dad. A Mrs. Parsons."

He looked at Mrs. Case. "Who's that? I know the name."

"That's that sour woman from the PTA," Mrs. Case reminded him. "I wonder what she could want?"

Sensing that the call had something to do with the accident, the family stood in the doorway of the den listening.

"Hello? Yes, of course I remember you. We've met you at PTA meetings," Mr. Case said smoothly, winking at his wife.

He listened quietly for a minute, a frown deepening at the corners of his mouth. They could hear Mrs. Parsons' sharp, high-pitched voice, and it was obvious she was angry about something. Finally Mr. Case said, "Yes, I heard the same thing from Vernon's mother, but don't you think we ought to investigate the matter thoroughly and hear what Sam has to say before taking a measure like that? . . . Oh, he has? Well, what does he say?"

Mrs. Case and the children edged into the room, hoping to hear the answer.

"Well then, that's all the more reason why we shouldn't act hastily." Mrs. Parsons' answer was so forceful that Mr.

Case had to hold the receiver away from his ear. His reply was polite but had the firm edge of a man dealing with an unreasonable person. "He may be a 'peril to the community,' as you call him, but as a member of the school board I would want to have all the facts in hand before voting for dismissal. If Sam says the brakes failed . . . Now, Mrs. Parsons, I assure you I'm taking this matter very seriously indeed. Vernon Stevenson happens to be a close friend of this family, and I do care about the lives of other children, so I'd appreciate it if you didn't speak to me in that tone."

David and Penny quietly applauded their father, but he waved them away.

"I'll tell you what I'll do," he said. "Since I'm an engineer, I'll be glad to undertake the technical side of the inquiry. We owe it to Sam and the children and ourselves to examine his claim about the brakes. Yes, I'll get on it at once. . . . Pardon me? . . . You're probably right, Mrs. Parsons, but if I may speak candidly, it would give me great personal satisfaction to prove you wrong."

He hung up sharply.

"She wants to fire Sam?" Mrs. Case said, touching her husband's arm.

"She wants to lynch him," he replied with a bitter smile. "She's talking about having him brought up on charges of criminal negligence, but she'll be satisfied if he's merely dismissed."

"Boy, you really went to bat for Sam," Penny said, hugging her father.

But he pulled away, his face troubled. "I didn't go to bat for Sam. I only went to bat for fair play. If Sam was indeed drinking, he'll get no sympathy from me. Perhaps 'peril to the community' is overdoing it, but I will not permit an irresponsible man to sit for five minutes behind the wheel of a school bus in this town, fond of Sam though I may be."

And he stormed out of the house, leaving his wife and children with their mouths open, as if a fleecy cloud had suddenly erupted into a violent thunderstorm.

3
Room 341

The nurse at the reception desk of Aubrey Park General Hospital looked up at the visitors and smiled. They had asked for Vernon Stevenson's room. She spun a large round index file, riffled through the *S*'s, and said, "Three-forty-one, on the third floor. There are two visitors up there now. Use that elevator over there."

Penny and David started to walk away. Then David remembered something. "Sam Gilman, where is he?"

"Three-fifty-six, but I'm afraid he can't have visitors today. He's still under sedation."

"Sedation?" asked Penny.

"Drugs," the nurse explained. "To kill the pain and calm him."

David and Penny thanked her and walked solemnly to the elevator. "He must really be in bad shape," David told his sister. Penny looked at her toes and fought back tears.

They got off at the third floor and followed numbered arrows down the spotless corridors of the hospital. Doctors and nurses in crisp white uniforms hurried past them on mysterious, urgent missions. An orderly in green was mopping a floor and looked crossly at them for marring his job with their footprints. An old man in a robe, obviously convalescing from an operation, shuffled painfully toward them and managed a small smile. A Puerto Rican family, consisting of father, mother, four children, and grandmother, milled outside one of the rooms. They had baskets of food and soda, candy, and flowers, and chattered laughingly in staccato Spanish, lending a strangely festive touch to the solemn, sterile hall. Farther up the corridor, three children were competing to see who could slide farthest on his knees on the polished floor. A stout nurse admonished them and they retreated timidly to a bench.

"You know what I hate about hospitals?" Penny said to her brother.

"What?"

"They're too clean. They're so clean they scare me."

"I know what you mean. But would you have them dirty?"

"Just a little messy to make them more human," Penny said.

They came to room 341. The door was half shut and they hesitated. Then they heard voices inside and tentatively pushed the door open. Vernon, in bright blue pajamas, was lying flat on his back except for his head, which was

wrapped in bandages and propped up slightly on a pillow. His right leg was packed in a huge white plaster cast from toe to thigh and suspended by a complicated system of cords, weights, and pulleys.

He was talking in a slurred, droning voice to someone just beyond David and Penny's vision, gesturing with his hands as if reenacting the accident. The children pushed the door open all the way to see who the other guests were.

"Ah, here they are!" said Ralph Carter, as if he had predicted their arrival.

"Come on in," his wife Lydia said warmly.

Although the Carters were adults, Penny and David and their friend Vernon felt as close to them as they did to people their own age. Ralph was their science teacher, and it was through him that they'd met Lydia, a lawyer who specialized in defending persons who could not afford attorneys' fees. The black couple had been very hospitable to the children, inviting them frequently to their home and responding sensitively to their needs and problems. Penny and David were thus not surprised that the Carters had taken time out of their busy schedules to visit Vernon.

Ralph went out into the hall to find two more chairs, and the children turned to Vernon. For several moments they could think of nothing but the pathetic sight of their friend lying injured and helpless, the same Vernon who a little more than twenty-four hours before was intense and full of vigor. Although he and David were the same age, thirteen, and Penny just a year younger, Vernon seemed to have aged fifty years. "That's what happens to geniuses," Lydia said, with a wry smile.

Vernon, face pale and eyelids droopy, smiled weakly and twiddled his fingers in greeting. David clutched the hand and gave it a little shake, but Penny finally succumbed to the tears that had been welling in her eyes all day long. Weeping, she leaned over the bed and kissed Vernon on the cheek.

A wave of bright red crept up Vernon's neck and suffused his face. "Wow," he murmured. "It's almost worth breaking my leg for this." His voice was nasal and his words blurred together, the result, the children surmised, of tranquilizers.

Penny, herself embarrassed by her impulse, wiped away her tears and held out a square gold box. "Chocolates," she announced, opening the gift wrapping and holding the open box in front of Vernon's nose. His mouth turned down.

"He can't eat anything right now," Lydia said. "He's still a bit nauseated from the medication they've been giving him."

Ralph came back with a couple of chairs. The four visitors sat down in a semicircle around the bed and for a moment squirmed in awkward silence, as if they were mourners at a funeral. Vernon himself broke the silence with, "What did you mean by 'That's what happens to geniuses,' Lydia?"

She grinned. "Simply that if you were of average intelligence like the rest of us, you'd have had the good sense to get off the bus when you were supposed to. What on earth was occupying you yesterday that you didn't even hear Sam call out your stop?"

"My newspaper turner," Vernon said.

After a moment of puzzled silence, Ralph Carter said, "All right, we'll bite. What's a newspaper turner?"

"Well, last week I was in New Manchester and had to take the bus back to Aubrey Park during rush hour. A lot of people were standing in the aisle trying to read the afternoon newspaper, but it was hard for them to turn the pages because everyone was crowded together. So I got this brainstorm . . ."

"And ended up in the hospital," Ralph finished for him. "A brainstorm is one thing, but brain damage is another."

"They don't think my brain is damaged," Vernon said, attempting a smile. "My father says I have the same screws loose now that I had before the accident."

Penny reached into the candy box and popped a chocolate into her mouth. She offered one to Lydia and Ralph. David helped himself.

"Can you talk about the accident?" David asked.

"Sure. I can tell you about it in one word: *boom!* One second I was on my seat and the next my seat was on me."

"You're a big help."

"What can I say? I never knew what hit me . . . no, that's not quite true. As I was telling Ralph and Lydia, I vaguely remember some unusual sounds just before the impact, but my head is so foggy with all the pills they've been giving me that I just can't bring anything into focus. One more good night's sleep ought to do it. Tell me, have you heard anything more about Sam? I know about his injuries, but I mean, has he said anything?"

They told their friend about Mrs. Parsons' phone call to their father in which she had said Sam claimed the brakes failed.

"Poor guy," Ralph said, clucking his tongue. "I guess he'll lose his job."

Lydia raised her eyebrows. Being a lawyer, and one who specialized in defending the poor, her husband's comment stirred a special response in her. "But if the brakes failed . . ."

"Sam is probably just saying that to get himself off the hook," Ralph replied. "After all, it was a brand-new bus, according to what I heard."

Lydia straightened in her seat and glared at her husband. "Why, Ralph Arthur Carter, I'd have expected more than that from a man with scientific training. You've condemned Sam without a shred of fact." If she hadn't softened her criticism with a look of affection, it might have started an angry quarrel.

Ralph lowered his eyes. "You're right. But put yourself in the shoes of the people on the school board. Do you think they'll buy Sam's story?"

Proudly, Penny said, "My father has bought it enough to block Sam's dismissal until the brakes have been examined."

"I'd like to shake your father's hand," Lydia said.

Tossing down several more chocolates, Penny added, "My father also says he won't have any sympathy for Sam if the inquiry finds Sam isn't telling the truth."

"Few people will," Lydia replied. "The public doesn't tolerate negligence or irresponsibility when children's lives are at stake. If Sam was drunk, he must be relieved of his duties."

"But what if it's just a matter of his getting a little old and his reflexes slowing? A man shouldn't be punished for that," David said, punctuating his sentence with a swipe at the chocolates.

"It depends on what you mean by punishment," Lydia said. "There are criminal-negligence laws which entitle the state to prosecute a man whose irresponsible actions result in injury to other persons or in property damage. So if Sam *was* drunk, the state could prosecute him if it wished. A second possibility is that he was not drunk, but as you say, David, because he's getting old or for some other reason, he made a misjudgment—went too fast, didn't see the red light, or the like. In that case, he wouldn't be subject to prosecution but might still be subject to dismissal. The school board, which is his employer, could rightfully claim that he is a menace to the children he's in charge of, as well as a threat to other people and property."

"But what if it's true that the brakes failed?" Penny said.

"Ah, that makes it interesting," Lydia said, reaching for a chocolate. "If the brakes failed we must find out why and who was responsible. Responsibility is a very important factor here, not just because we want to make sure that such brake failures don't happen again, but because somebody is going to owe somebody else money when the investigators get to the bottom of this thing."

"I don't understand," Penny said. "Do you mean lawsuits?"

"That's just what I mean. The school board, which owns the bus, wants to recover the cost of repairing or replacing it. The owner of the gardening truck wants to recover damages to his vehicle and to the trees it was carrying. The supermarket may try to recover money for damages it suffered."

"Don't forget me," Vernon reminded Lydia feebly.

"I was saving the best for last," the lawyer answered. "Vernon's parents will undoubtedly want to sue for the medical expenses they incur putting our Humpty Dumpty together again. So it's vital to fix the responsibility."

"I'm beginning to see," David said, and turned to his sister to explain it. "If they find that Sam was negligent, then his employer, the school board, is the responsible party and has to pay for all the damages. But if someone else was responsible—say, the garage which is supposed to inspect the bus's brakes—then *that* party gets sued."

"Right," said Lydia. "So this inquiry is going to prove very important to a lot of people."

"I think Vernon cares more about getting some sleep than winning a lawsuit," Ralph said, getting to his feet and motioning for the others to do the same.

Vernon's eyes, which were almost closed, widened for a moment. "I'm sorry to be rude, but these drugs . . . Listen, before you go, will you do me two favors?"

"Sure," Penny said eagerly.

"First, I want you all to sign your names on my cast. There's a pen over here by my telephone."

Penny found the pen and the four visitors wrote encouraging little remarks on the cast and signed their names.

"The other thing is, next time you come, David or Penny, will you bring me the items listed on the piece of paper on my telephone table? Most of the stuff is in my basement. If you have to buy the rest of it, I'll pay you for it—out of the million dollars I win in my lawsuit."

Penny picked up the paper. She studied it for a moment, her mouth forming a quizzical pucker. "Electric motor, one-inch pulley, three-inch pulley, clamps, cord . . . Vernon, what on earth is all this for?"

"It's too complicated to explain," he said.

"I can explain it," David laughed. "Vernon's gone off his nut."

"Yes," Ralph said, "I think we'll have to pack a screwdriver with all that gear. I'm afraid there are more screws loose in that head of his than we thought."

"Don't worry, I know what I'm doing," he said, waving good-bye to them. Just as they were filing out of the room, he called Penny's name. "One more thing. Can I have one of those chocolates you brought? I have this awful taste in my mouth."

Penny went to the window ledge where she'd left the box. She opened it and gulped. "Oh, my! I don't know how to tell you this, but . . . we ate them all."

"Thanks a lot," Vernon moaned, falling into a doze.

Sleep swept over him like a warm wave, but it was neither a deep sleep nor a restful one. Voices in the corridor mingled with strange dreams to create a tortured fantasia, as if he had drifted into an abstract painting. His conscious mind struggled for supremacy over his unconscious one—the one that kept producing these grotesque, unwelcome images. Suddenly his mind was replaying the accident. He was leaning over in the back seat of the bus, using the seat next to him as a desk. The bus tilted downward, indicating they were beginning to descend a hill. Vernon thought this strange, since there was no hill on the route to his stop, but he didn't want to take his eyes off his sketch. The bus seemed to be picking up speed, and then . . . sounds. What were they? "Think, Vernon," he commanded himself, but his mind was flooded with other sounds, ranging from television jingles to nurses' orders.

He tried to control all these random impressions, clearing away everything but that bus ride. Yes, there they were: *Stamp . . . hiss . . . honk.* Those were the sounds. *Stamp,* like someone jumping on the floor of the bus. *Hiss,* like air rushing out of a tube. *Honk,* like an automobile horn. *Stamp . . . hiss . . . honk. Stamp . . . hiss . . . honk.*

All at once something was intruding on his dream. Something was telling him to wake up. He opened his eyelids just a crack. As he did he heard *Stamp . . . hiss . . . honk!*

"What on earth?" he muttered.

Vernon turned his head toward the door. There, in a wheelchair, was Sam Gilman. He wore a hospital gown, his left arm was in a cast suspended from his neck in a sling, and his head was bandaged. His face was pale and unshaven and his eyes were rimmed with black, blue, and yellow bruises.

Now Vernon understood what the noises were. The stamping sound had been Sam knocking on the door, and the hiss and honk were Sam going, "*Pssst,* Vernon."

"Sam, what are you doing here?"

Sam put his finger over his lips and wheeled his chair into the room. "I had to speak to you, son. I wanted to tell you how god-awful sorry I am about this."

"It's all right, Sam. These things happen."

"No, they don't 'happen.' Nothing like that ever happened to me, and I've been driving since before you were born."

"Nothing like what ever happened to you?"

"I mean brake failure, son. I've seen 'em gradually fade out over a period of time—that's one thing. But one second they're on and the next they're off—that I've never seen. That I've never even heard of." Vernon started to speak, but Sam said, "Listen to me, the nurse will be coming after me, so I got to talk fast. I know people are saying I was drunk. Son, may the good Lord strike me down with a thunderbolt if I'm lying when I tell you I've never touched a drop on the job since I've been a driver. Heck, you've been a rider with me for eight or nine years. You *know* how much I love the kids. Why, I'd sooner quit than see a hair on their heads . . ."

Tears were welling up in his eyes. He probably would have burst into sobs had not a nurse and an orderly barged into the room. "There you are!" the nurse growled. "What do you think this is, the Indianapolis 500? Back you go, mister, and if I hear of you climbing out of that bed once more without doctor's orders, I'm going to tie you in."

She winked at Vernon, indicating she wasn't as serious as all that, and the orderly turned Sam around and wheeled him out of the room. Sam looked over his shoulder and cried, "You got to believe me, son. Those brakes just gave flat out."

"I do believe you, Sam," Vernon shouted back. But that cold, logical corner of Vernon's brain had a different answer. It said, "I'll decide when the evidence is in."

4

A Painful Duty

"Don't touch that!"

Mr. Case, who had left the dining room to make a phone call, returned sooner than Penny had expected, catching her peeking into the manila folder he had left beside his plate. His voice was stern, not tempered by fatherly affection as it usually was when he scolded her.

He had been solemn and jumpy ever since coming down to breakfast, clutching the folder tightly as if afraid it would leap out of his hands if he relaxed his grip. Even Mrs. Case had noticed and looked at him questioningly when she placed his food before him. But whatever was bothering him, he was apparently not going to share it with his wife. That made this a very serious matter indeed, for Mr. and Mrs.

Case talked *everything* over between them. She signaled her children to leave their father alone until he was ready to share what was troubling him with his family.

Of course, they had more than an inkling of what it was. Today, two weeks after the accident, was the day of the school-board hearing to determine the cause. Mr. Case had spent a great deal of that time away from his job in an effort to make a thorough, accurate, and fair analysis of the bus's brakes. He had supervised tests, contacted other engineers, examined the brakes himself, and had even taken the bus for a short ride to ascertain whether or not there was any truth to Sam's claim.

The answer was in that folder he'd brought to breakfast. All during the past week Penny and David had been asking him what he'd learned, but he would only repeat what he had told them at the outset—that he had promised the board he'd discuss the case with no one until he had presented the facts at the hearing. The purpose of this rule was to ensure a fair investigation. If the news leaked out prematurely, it might give an advantage to one of the interested parties.

This approach made good sense, yet Penny and David couldn't understand how their father could exclude his own flesh and blood. They had pestered him continually, promising they would never speak a word of what they learned to anyone, but it was to no avail.

And now Penny had gone so far as to try to sneak a look at the folder while her father was out of the room.

Frowning, Mr. Case snatched up the folder, gulped down the rest of his coffee, and left the house without saying good-bye to anybody.

Penny and David looked up at their mother. "Why is he so grouchy today?" Penny asked.

"He's feeling guilty," Mrs. Case said.

"Guilty?"

"About having to perform an unpleasant task," Mrs. Case answered, and retreated into the kitchen, leaving her children wondering.

The hearing was being held in the teachers' lounge of the Aubrey Park Elementary School. The room was spacious and bright and the air filled with the rich aroma of fresh coffee brewed in a large urn near the windows. Yet there was no gaiety reflected in the twenty or so faces that turned to Mr. Case as he entered. "I'll bet there are a lot of other children this morning wondering what's gotten into their parents," he said grimly to himself.

The chairs were arranged in a semicircle around a table at which sat Mr. Gainor, the school's principal; Mr. Twilly, school-board chairman; and four other officers of the board, including Mrs. Parsons representing the PTA.

In a corner, looking frightened and isolated, was Sam Gilman, who had been released from the hospital for the morning to attend the hearing. He sat in a wheelchair, his head bandaged and his arm in a sling. Behind him stood a chubby middle-aged man who appeared to be a friend. They talked in low tones, surveying the faces in the room as if assessing how sympathetic each one might be. Their eyes focused for a second on Mr. Case, who felt a sharp twinge in his stomach and turned his eyes away.

Mr. Twilly motioned to Mr. Case to join them at the table.

Uneasily, he lowered himself into a chair, undid the string on his folder, and removed a sheaf of papers. Mrs. Parsons, sitting beside him, leaned over to look at them, but he shielded them from her view with his arm. Her lips tightened and she turned away.

Mr. Twilly looked at his watch, then signaled to a woman sitting near the door to close it. The tension in the room began to rise at once, as if sealed in.

Mr. Twilly cleared his throat, called for order, and then said, "Ladies and gentlemen, we are meeting here to try to determine the cause of the bus accident of Tuesday, April 17th, involving Sam Gilman. This is not a trial, but an informal inquiry to sort out conflicting accounts of how the accident happened and who was responsible for it. But although this is not a legal proceeding, it is still a very important and serious one. If we find that the charge of recklessness leveled at Sam Gilman has merit, it may not only result in some sort of disciplinary action or dismissal, but could lead to civil or even criminal legal action. On the other hand, if Sam's claim that the brakes failed is true, proceedings will be instituted to find out why they failed and who is at fault."

Mr. Twilly reviewed the accident, and upon completing his summary produced a piece of paper containing the testimony of Merton Pringle, the old man who had witnessed the accident. He read the testimony and then turned his eyes to a gray-haired gentleman who sat ramrod-straight in military fashion at the back of the room. "Mr. Pringle, would you mind coming forward so that we can ask you a few questions?"

Pringle rose and walked to the front of the room.

"Mr. Pringle, when the police questioned you, you told

them you thought Sam Gilman was drunk. On what did you base your assertion?"

Mr. Pringle shrugged as if the answer was obvious. "Why, just from the way he drove. Nobody would go down that hill as fast as he was going unless he was under the influence of alcohol—and a lot of it. But what convinced me was the look on his face as he drove past me. He was grinning as if it was a hilarious joke."

Sam's mouth dropped open, and he muttered something to his companion.

Mr. Twilly seemed to guess what Sam had said, and asked the witness, "Couldn't that look on his face have been a grimace of terror?"

Mr. Pringle thought for a moment and agreed that it could have been.

"Was there anything else that led you to conclude that Sam was drunk? Think carefully, sir; this is extremely important. Was he holding a liquor bottle or something like that?"

"No, not really," he answered with a subdued air.

Mr. Twilly opened a file folder. "According to the police, a thorough search of the bus after the accident produced no liquor bottle or anything else that might have contained liquor. They also searched Sam's locker but found nothing that might suggest he'd been drinking. Most significant of all is a report prepared by the laboratory at Aubrey Park General Hospital. They checked a sample of Sam Gilman's blood shortly after he was admitted, and determined that there was no alcohol content whatever."

There was a murmur throughout the room, and it seemed to be one of satisfaction, as if everyone had been hoping that

Sam would be vindicated. Sam brightened, and a trace of a smile flickered across his mouth. But it faded quickly as he looked at the people behind the table. None of the board members seemed the least bit relieved. Indeed, Mr. Case looked more ill at ease than before, and Mrs. Parsons was scowling.

It was Mr. Pringle who set the tone for what was to follow. As he got up to return to his seat he said, "Well, if the man wasn't drunk, he must have been out of his mind."

Mr. Twilly looked irritated. "I hope we can disregard that remark," he said to the little assembly. "There is a more logical explanation of Sam's behavior, and that is the one that Sam himself has provided us with. Namely, that the bus's brakes failed. Therefore our next order of business will be to hear from Mr. Edward Case. Mr. Case is a member of this board and an engineer and has volunteered to investigate the technical angle. Ed?"

For a moment Mr. Case appeared to be glued to his seat. Then he rose tiredly. He opened his folder and stared at it for a minute, as if hoping that its contents had been miraculously transformed since he had last looked at it. Then he began to speak quietly.

"After the accident," Mr. Case began, "the bus, a one-month-old Federal Motors model 6300, was towed to the Mulberry Street police garage. The first opportunity I had to examine it was the evening of the day after the accident, when I returned home from work. Although the steel shell of the bus was seriously damaged, the wheels and their brake structure did not seem to have been affected by the impact. But of course, we couldn't be sure until we tried the brakes. I had the police pry away a fender that was interfering with the front wheels, so that the bus could move freely. I then drove the bus a few yards while still in the garage and tried the brakes."

Everyone leaned forward to hear his next words, which Mr. Case seemed to have difficulty getting out of his throat.

"And?" prompted Mr. Twilly.

"They worked. Perfectly."

A ripple of shock swept across the room. There was a moment of silence and then Sam Gilman spoke. "No! No, that's just not possible. I pumped them right down to the floor. Nothing happened, not a blessed thing. You must be mistaken, Mr. Case."

Mr. Case could not look at Sam. Mr. Twilly interjected, "Now, Sam, Mr. Case is just doing his job. You mustn't take his conclusions personally."

But Sam was too upset to control himself. "Personally? Why, how else can I take it? It's being suggested that I'm a liar, that I drove recklessly like Pringle said."

Everyone in the room shifted uncomfortably in his chair. Mr. Twilly was calm and tactful but also firm. "Sam," he said with obvious affection, "you know that all of us here were hoping Mr. Case's investigation would prove you right. But the facts do speak for themselves." He turned to Mr. Case. "Do you have anything to add, Ed?"

Mr. Case looked down at his papers and said, "Just more of the same, I'm afraid. I took the bus out into the parking lot behind the police garage and drove it at increasing speeds. The brakes worked every time. I even had them sprayed with water because sometimes brakes will slip when they're wet, but that didn't make any difference, and besides, it hadn't rained for a week before the accident, so there were no puddles along Sam's route. Finally, I took the bus up to the hill on Temple Avenue and drove it down five times at speeds ranging from ten to fifty miles per hour. The brakes," he concluded in an almost inaudible voice, "worked perfectly each time."

Sam was shaking his head in bewilderment. "I must be losing my mind," he mumbled. His friend behind him put a restraining hand on his shoulder.

Suddenly Mrs. Parsons rose and, in her sharp voice, said, "I'd like to say something about that."

The faces of a number of people betrayed distaste. It was obvious that Mrs. Parsons was not very popular. Even Mr. Twilly seemed reluctant to ask her to speak, but she looked determined to have her say whether he invited her or not. "Mrs. Parsons?"

Mrs. Parsons' face was stern. "My friends, we have heard two important facts brought out here today. The first is that Sam Gilman was not drunk. The second is that the bus brakes did work. What, then, can we conclude? I say, only one thing, the thing that Sam himself has just suggested. Maybe 'out of his mind' is putting it strongly, but can anyone here honestly say that a man in his right mind would drive a school bus the way Sam drove that day? Even if he believed there were no children in it, he still endangered the lives of pedestrians and other motorists, as well as vehicles and property. He also endangered his own life, and I've been wondering if maybe that's just what he had in mind."

Mr. Twilly's face registered astonishment. "Mrs. Parsons, are you suggesting that Sam was . . ."

"I'm not afraid to say it, Mr. Twilly: trying to commit suicide."

Several people began to mutter angrily to one another, but Mrs. Parsons didn't flinch. She waited for the furor to subside.

"Mrs. Parsons," said Mr. Twilly, his voice trembling, "unless you are prepared to support your charge I'm going to demand you apologize to Sam."

"I'll do no such thing, sir. I'm only saying what I believe everyone here is thinking and is afraid to say. But I *can* support my charge. I've been conducting a little investigation of my own. I've spoken to a lot of parents and children in the last week. A number of them have told me that Sam has not been himself for the last few months. He used to joke with everybody—something, by the way, I've never approved of, because a man should pay strict attention to what he's doing —but, at any rate, lately he's been glum and even surly. And he's been late picking up children. And I've heard a few other things I won't bother going into, but which say to me that Sam's been behaving irrationally."

People were listening to Mrs. Parsons now, but their faces indicated skepticism. Mr. Twilly's question reflected what they were thinking. "Isn't it possible that Sam merely had some sort of personal trouble on his mind, as all of us do at one time or another? I don't believe, Mrs. Parsons, that you are justified in jumping to the conclusion that because something may have been bothering Sam, he would try to do away with himself." Mr. Twilly turned to Sam and was about to ask him to reply to Mrs. Parsons' remarks, but Mrs. Parsons never gave him a chance.

"If that's all there were to it, Mr. Twilly, I would agree with you. But there is something else. Something far more serious."

Mr. Twilly took several deep breaths and said, "And what is that?"

"I have learned that Sam has been in the care of a psychiatrist for the past six months." Triumphantly she waved a piece of paper, saying, "His name is right here if anyone wants to check for himself."

"Oh, God, not that!" Sam gasped, his head dropping to his chest.

For a moment there was absolute silence.

"Sam," the chairman said gently, "can you explain?"

Sam tried to pull himself together, but he seemed completely beaten. "I—I—oh, what's the use? Get me out of here, Ken."

"But Sam, you can't let things stand this way," his friend pleaded. "You've got to defend yourself."

"It wouldn't do any good. They've made up their minds. Get me out of here."

"Sam . . ." his friend tried again.

"*Get me out of here!*" he cried, and his friend, muttering apologies, wheeled Sam abruptly out of the room.

Mr. Case jumped to his feet and pointed a finger at Mrs. Parsons. "That was cruel and unnecessary."

"It had to be said," she replied with a sniff.

"It could have been said with Sam out of the room. We're not here to crucify him, you know."

"We're here to see that justice is done and our children's lives protected," she replied.

Mr. Twilly shouted them down. "Can we have some order here?" Still glaring at each other, Mr. Case and Mrs. Parsons sat down. "I don't approve of the way Mrs. Parsons handled this matter either, but what's done is done, and perhaps

it's all for the best. We must come to a decision about a course of action. Will those parents who are not members of the school board and who came merely as observers kindly leave the room so that we can make a determination?" About a dozen persons filed out of the room, and after the door was shut, Mr. Twilly said, "I'll now entertain the board's proposals."

Mr. Gainor rose to his feet. "I'm tremendously upset about what I've seen and heard this morning. But I don't think we can let our sympathy for Sam get in the way of our obligation to the community, and especially the children. Therefore I'm reluctantly compelled to move that this board relieve Sam of his job, effective at once."

"I second the motion," Mrs. Parsons snapped.

"Is there any discussion?" Mr. Twilly asked. No one raised a hand. "Then we'll vote on the motion, namely, that Sam Gilman be dismissed at once. All in favor?"

One by one and heavily, as if burdened with lead weights, the hands of the school-board members went up. The first was Mrs. Parsons', the last Mr. Case's.

"Then it's unanimous," Mr. Twilly said wearily. "Sam Gilman is to be dismissed. I will notify him at once. This meeting is over."

5
A Question
of Workmanship

"Here's the rest of it," David announced, pushing the door to Vernon's room open with his hip because his arms were loaded down with two grocery bags.

"*Shhh,* not so loud," Vernon cautioned him. "If the nurses knew what I was doing . . ."

"If *I* knew what you were doing!" David replied, dropping the bags on the bed near his friend's plaster-encased foot. "Last time it was wheels and pulleys and cord and electric motors; this time it's chains and gears and—"

"You'll understand soon enough, but first we've got to hide this stuff before the nurse comes. I've got the first package in the laundry hamper underneath the plastic liner, but I doubt if we can get these two in there." They fell silent, looking about the room for a suitable hiding place. Vernon's eyes finally fixed on a narrow locker that said *Oxygen*. "See if there's an oxygen bottle in there."

David opened it. "Nope, no bottle." Hastily he shoved the two grocery bags into the locker, then got the third package out of the laundry hamper and put it in the locker too. "Now, will you kindly tell me what this is all about?"

"Sure. I'm going to— *Shut the locker!*"

David slammed the door shut just as a stout nurse poked her head in the door and looked at him with squinty-eyed suspicion. David stood with his back to the locker looking up at the ceiling innocently. "This is a hospital, not a playground, boys," she growled.

"I beg your pardon?" David said politely.

"Don't beg my pardon, just behave. I have four like you at home and I *always* know what they're up to."

"Yes, ma'am," the boys said in concert.

"Now, if you wouldn't mind stepping outside for a few minutes, young man, I have to change this fellow's sheets."

David left the room and closed the door behind him. He took a seat on a bench in the corridor and for several minutes watched the endlessly interesting hospital scene pass before his eyes. Doctors, nurses, orderlies, technicians, convalescents, pregnant women, patients in wheelchairs or on wheeled beds, and visitors, visitors, visitors. With each person who went by, David's thoughts and emotions took a different turn. The sight of an expectant mother stimulated pleasant visions of newborn babies and happy parents; then he'd be plunged into depression as an old, shriveled woman was wheeled down the hall.

He looked at his watch and wondered where Penny was.

She was supposed to have met him in the hospital lobby, but after waiting ten minutes he'd given up and gone on without her. Just as Vernon's door opened again, Penny turned the corner and waved to her brother. The nurse emerged, shook her finger at David, and said, "Remember."

"We'll remember," David said sweetly, and the nurse strode away.

"What was that all about?" Penny asked as they stepped into Vernon's room.

"Mrs. Minster seems to think David and I are up to something," the patient said.

"How could she suspect such a thing, knowing what good little boys you two are?" Penny said sarcastically.

"They call her Minster the Monster," Vernon told them, and they laughed.

David shook his head. "It's true we're up to something, but Vernon won't tell me what it is."

"I'll explain later, but first tell me what happened at the hearing this morning."

"My dad wouldn't give me many details," said David, "but it looks like Sam is going to be fired."

"Then he *was* drunk," Vernon said, shaking his head with amazement.

"No, that's the strange part. He was sober but drove recklessly for some other reason, and my dad won't tell me what it is."

"That *is* strange. But what about Sam's claim that the brakes failed?"

David lowered his eyes and shrugged. "My dad says it's impossible. He tested them in every conceivable way and they worked perfectly every time."

A rarely seen look came over Vernon's face. It was one of anger. "And Sam swore up and down that those brakes failed," he said bitterly.

"He did?" David asked.

"Yes. He came into my room the day after the accident and begged me to believe him. And I did. But now I find out that I'm cooped up in this place with a broken leg because he decided to take a joyride in his bus."

David and Penny, unaccustomed to such strength of feeling from their normally easygoing friend, backed away a step. Penny offered a consoling word. "Well, what's done is done. You'll be out of here before long and you'll be good as new."

"It's not my leg so much as my faith in people," Vernon said. "I never figured Sam would lie to me."

His disappointment seemed to drop an invisible curtain between the boy and his visitors, and David decided that further discussion of the accident would be bad for Vernon's state of mind. Seeking to bring cheer back into the room, he turned to his sister and said, "Well now, young lady, where have you been? You were supposed to be here at four."

"I was over at Gilroy's getting my bike fixed."

"Why'd it take so long?"

"Oh, he was talking my ear off about the decline of workmanship in this country."

Vernon brightened. The subject was one that interested him. The curtain that had momentarily isolated him seemed to lift. "What about it?"

"Well, it started because that brand-new chain he put on three days ago snapped. I was really mad and brought the bike down there and was going to insist he repair it for free.

But I didn't have to; he offered to replace it without charge. Then he started talking about how hard it is to get well-manufactured goods nowadays. In the old days, things were built to last, but today a lot of people who work in factories don't seem to care that much, or their bosses care more about profits than quality. There's no more pride in what they do, so they get sloppy and turn out products that break the first time you use them, like my chain."

"Maybe today's factory worker has it too easy. He's well paid and has so many fringe benefits that he's become lazy," Vernon said.

"You wouldn't want to return to the days of the sweatshop, would you, when men and women and even children worked ten hours a day, six or seven days a week in the most horrible conditions?" David pointed out.

"I think Mr. Gilroy would," Penny said. "He's really up in arms about this workmanship business. He says scarcely a day goes by when he doesn't return a faulty item to the manufacturer. He inspects everything as carefully as he can, but the weak link in my chain must have got by him. What makes him so mad is that poorly made products aren't merely a nuisance, but a danger as well. Suppose my chain had snapped as I was applying my brakes at an intersection!"

"Maybe machines are the answer," Vernon suggested. "We've developed machines that can do almost any human job, and do it better, so why shouldn't machines be able to turn out products of as high quality as human laborers?"

"Vernon thinks machines are the answer to everything," Penny teased.

"At least they don't sass you the way some girls do," Vernon retorted. "And speaking of machines, I was going to tell David about all these tools and parts I've had him bring here all week long. You see . . . uh-oh, the Monster."

Nurse Minster stuck her head in the door. "You'll have to clear out, kids. The doctor will be here in a second and I want to take Vernon's temperature." David and Penny did not care to tangle with this formidable woman and backed out of the room submissively.

"And I still don't know what all those gadgets are for," David lamented as he pushed the elevator button.

After the doctor had examined him and left, Vernon slid down in his bed, put his hands behind his head, and let his mind wander. It wandered in many directions, from Sam Gilman's lie to Penny's difficulty with her bicycle chain to the tools and parts stowed in the oxygen locker. But one word kept flashing on and off in his brain: workmanship.

Until a few hours before, Vernon had been working on figuring out how the bus's brakes could have failed. Then when David had told him Sam's story was a lie, for a while Vernon had been outraged. But now he was calm and determined not to let his emotions interfere with his thinking. He recalled Sam's appearance in his room that day, when Sam pleaded with him to believe the brakes had failed. Vernon had been moved, and he now began to wonder whether anything so touching could have been an act. But if Sam was not acting that day, if the brakes did fail as he was claiming—how come they worked when Mr. Case tested them?

Penny's remarks about shoddy workmanship on her bicycle chain had revived his interest in the subject, and a fascinating question now began to form in his mind. Could a brake fail on one occasion and work on another?

With some difficulty, because his leg was still in traction, Vernon reached the telephone. He dialed the Cases' number and got David. "Hi, it's me. I wonder if you'd do me a favor."

"Sure," David said. "What is it?"

"I'd like you to go to the library and bring me whatever you can find on automotive engineering—the more technical, the better. Can you drop the books off tomorrow?"

There was a long pause. "Vernon, are you sure your brain wasn't damaged in that accident?"

"I don't think it was. Why?"

"Because I don't think the hospital administration is going to look kindly on your plan to build an automobile in your room."

Vernon laughed. "Don't worry, I'm not building an automobile."

"Then what *are* you building?"

Vernon smiled. "A theory, David. I'm building a theory."

6

Another Accident!

Vernon slammed the fat book shut and shoved it away. "The last one was too simple, but this one is too technical. I'd have to have a degree in engineering to understand what I just read," he grumbled to no one in particular. He collected the seven books he'd been poring over in bed and put them in a paper shopping bag, one of the items he'd had David bring him. He now hooked the handles of the book-filled bag over a length of picture wire he and David had stretched from the bed to a corner of the room. Vernon gave the bag a gentle shove, and it slid down the wire and parked with a bump against the wall to his right. Attached to the bag was a string whose other end was safety-pinned to his bedsheet so that he could retrieve the books with a tug.

He raised his eyes and was startled to discover he was not alone. His father was standing in the doorway, along with a slim man in a three-piece suit whom Vernon had never seen before. And behind them, looking as cross as a vulture, stood Nurse Minster.

Dr. Stevenson shook his head affectionately. "Vernon, can't you ever stop inventing things?"

"I guess not. But it was you who told me the devil finds mischief for idle hands."

His father looked with amazement at a few of the devices Vernon had rigged up in his hospital room. "The devil wouldn't have a chance here," he said proudly. Then he turned to the man behind him. "Vernon, I'd like you to meet an old friend of mine, Dr. Philbin. Dr. Philbin is attending a convention in New Manchester, and I thought that as long as he is in town he wouldn't mind having a look at you."

"A look . . . ?"

"He's a brain specialist," Dr. Stevenson explained as Dr. Philbin stepped forward.

"Don't worry," the slim doctor said with a smile. "I doubt if there's anything wrong with your brain. Anyone who has managed to put all this together is in complete control of his faculties," he said with an admiring wave of the hand. Nurse Minster uttered a grunt of disapproval. "Still, it wouldn't hurt to have a look at you," he said, sitting down on the bed.

"Shall I remove the bandage from his head, doctor?" the nurse asked.

"No, I'll do it myself. Just crank the patient's bed up to a sitting position, if you don't mind."

"Certainly." Nurse Minster stepped to the foot of the bed and stooped, but just as she was about to begin cranking, she was startled by a humming sound. She jumped back as the crank started turning by itself, raising Vernon automatically to a sitting position. The boy had a button in his hand and a grin on his face.

"Just thought I'd save you some work," he said.

"See if you can invent an automatic paddle for spanking mischievous boys," she said, retreating to the doorway with a sour expression.

"Not a bad idea at all. I'll think about it."

Dr. Philbin finished unwinding the bandage on Vernon's head and examined the place on his brow, just below the hairline, that had struck the metal seat in front of him when the bus crashed. "Well, you'll be going through life with a nice little dent, I'm afraid, but it will hardly be noticeable. The scar where they stitched you up will look a little gruesome at first, but that will fade over the years until it's just a thin line. It ought to blend with the other wrinkles in your forehead when you get older." He turned to Dr. Stevenson. "I'll run a few simple tests now to check his vision, hearing, reflexes, and motor abilities. If I find anything out of order . . . well, we can take it from there."

He proceeded to prod and poke Vernon, make him read an eye chart, ask him to move fingers and toes and joints, whisper questions to him at various distances to test his hearing, and perform various other tests to get a general idea of how well Vernon's brain was functioning.

"I don't find anything wrong," he said to Dr. Stevenson, who sighed with relief, "but if he complains of headaches, dizziness, blurred vision, ringing in his ears, or any of the other symptoms we talked about before, call me at once." He turned to Nurse Minster. "And he's not to be paddled, tempt-

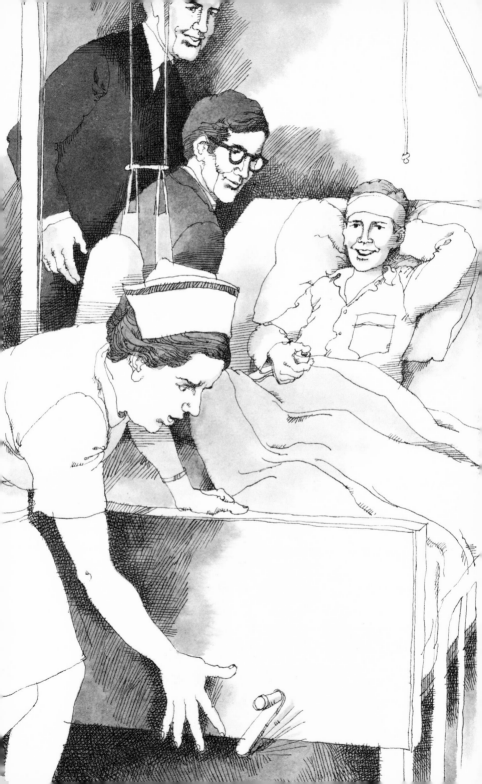

ing though such an idea may be."

She suppressed a smile. "Yes, doctor."

They left and Vernon reached for the button to activate the electric motor which he and David had installed to raise or lower the bed without having to bother the busy nurse. Instead of the button, however, his hand fell on a newspaper. He picked it up and examined the front page. It was the *Verona Ledger,* Dr. Philbin's hometown paper. He had left it behind accidentally. Vernon almost rang for Nurse Minster to see if she could catch Dr. Philbin, but decided to leave her alone until her displeasure with him had cooled a bit.

So curious was Vernon about everything that he would read an out-of-town newspaper just to see if it added anything to his knowledge of the world. This one didn't seem likely to, being mostly concerned with small-town local events. Then a headline on page seven jumped out at him: "School Bus Mishap Injures Six." Quickly he scanned the article.

> The driver and five children were injured, none of them seriously, when a school bus carrying thirty-two children to Verona Central School struck the rear end of an automobile stopped at a red light. None of the three occupants of the car was hurt, and damage to the two vehicles was minor. The injured children were treated at Coral Park Hospital and released. The bus driver, Clifford Morgan of 3205 Axminster Street, is being questioned by school and police officials in an effort to determine the cause of the accident.

The instant he finished, Vernon reached over his head and yanked a cord connected, through a system of pulleys, to a tray at the side of his bed. On the tray sat the telephone, and when Vernon tugged, the tray swung directly in front of him.

His first call was to David and Penny. He got Penny and read the article to her. Her reaction was the same as Vernon's: wild excitement. Perhaps the Verona and Aubrey Park accidents were a coincidence, but there was enough similarity to merit a closer look.

"What are you going to do?" Penny asked.

"Find out everything I can about the other accident, maybe even try to get in touch with the driver. His address is right here: Clifford Morgan of 3205 Axminster Street. I especially want to know the name of the manufacturer of the bus, what year and model it was, and most important of all, the lot number of the brakes."

"What's a lot number?"

"The brakes are made in batches," Vernon explained, "which are called lots. I want to find out if the lot number of the Verona bus's brakes is the same as that of the brakes on Sam Gilman's bus."

"I see. If it's the same manufacturer, and the lot numbers are identical . . ."

"We'll know that whatever went wrong with Sam's brakes went wrong with the other bus's as well."

"Then you've gone back to believing Sam's story?" Penny asked.

"Let's establish the facts and Sam's story will take care of itself. I'll have to work as fast as possible. If there are other school buses driving around with faulty brakes, we don't have a moment to spare."

Vernon's second call was to Lydia Carter at her office in New Manchester. Her answering service told him Mrs. Carter was in court. Vernon left a message asking her to call him the moment she returned. He urgently wanted to see her and her husband.

He pushed the telephone away and pulled the cord attached to the bag containing those automotive books. "I'm going to understand how brakes work if it takes me all night," he vowed, taking the fat book out of the bag.

7
Strategy Meeting

"Lemonade?" Lydia asked David and Penny that evening when they returned to the Carter home after visiting the hospital.

"Why ask?" Ralph laughed, lowering himself into his favorite armchair. "You know what their answer will be."

"That's true," Lydia said, disappearing into the kitchen. The air was filled with the pleasant sounds of ice being removed from trays, lemons being juiced in a machine, and a pitcher being filled. In a few moments she returned with the frosty pitcher and four glasses.

A minute went by during which there was nothing but the sounds of sipping and gurgles of satisfaction. Then Ralph said to his two young friends, "Well, what do you think?"

Penny was the first to answer. "I think if Vernon's right, this bus business could be of real importance."

"*Do* you think he's right?" Ralph followed up.

"She always thinks Vernon is right," David said, teasing his sister with a flutter of the eyelids.

Penny's face grew pink, but she ignored her brother's remark. "The coincidence between the two accidents is amazing, but we don't know enough yet to say whether both were caused by the same defect."

"Very true," Ralph said. "You may be making a statistical error. Out of, let's say, a thousand identical buses involved in the same kind of accident, there are bound to be a number of different causes. You've got to get all the information possible about the two buses as well as about any other buses involved in similar accidents. Let's assume that Sam's bus and the Verona bus are both made by the same company and their brake-lot numbers are identical. What if, when they test the brakes on the Verona bus, they work perfectly just as they did on Sam Gilman's bus?"

"Then we're back where we started," Penny admitted.

"Unless," David qualified, "we can find what it is about those brakes that makes them work normally one day and fail the next and go back to working normally again. But to do that we'd have to get hold of a set of brakes from that lot and take them apart. They'd have to be examined by a qualified automotive engineer and . . . well, that sort of thing can get pretty expensive."

"I have an idea," Penny piped up. "Why don't we just write to the company or companies that made the buses and ask them to send us a diagram of their brakes?"

Lydia entered the conversation. "I'm afraid that isn't too

realistic. The construction of their brakes is probably a trade secret which they would not want to give out."

Ralph had been whirling the ice cubes around his glass as his wife spoke, as if trying to shake loose a good idea. Now he jiggled the glass like an alarm bell. "They might not give out blueprints, but I don't think they'd mind talking generally about their brakes. You know, the eastern headquarters of Federal Motors is right downtown in New Manchester, and their public relations department is always entertaining groups of students. Why don't we make this a Science Club research project? I'll call them and tell them you two would like to talk to them. Public relations people are usually pretty eager to please the public and discuss their products. They feel it creates good will among potential buyers."

"Don't count me among them," Penny said indignantly. "If that's the way they make brakes, I certainly don't want to ride around in any vehicles they make."

"Don't be too quick to condemn them," Lydia said. One of the amazing things about Lydia was that she could be as fair to a multimillion-dollar corporation as she was to a poverty-stricken individual. "As things stand right now, I'm by no means convinced they make bad brakes. We don't know if Federal Motors was the manufacturer of the Verona bus. We still don't even know whether that second bus accident was caused by brake failure or drunkenness or some child hitting the driver in the back of the head with a tennis racket. Or if there is a defect in their brakes, they may not be aware of it. Maybe this particular lot is the only one they've ever produced with a flaw in it. Once a company like that knows there is a technical problem in its products, it is usually very quick to respond; Federal Motors doesn't want a lot of expensive lawsuits on its hands. *But*—you will have to convince them there *is* a technical problem, convince them beyond a shadow of a doubt. If I may speak as a lawyer, your case doesn't have a leg to stand on without hard facts."

"I guess our work is cut out for us," David said, a faint vibration of discouragement in his voice.

"I propose we work on several fronts at the same time to make our task easier," Ralph said. "While Penny and David are visiting Federal Motors, Vernon can be writing the motor vehicle bureaus of this and other states to find out if there have been other school bus accidents of the Aubrey Park and Verona type, and if so, what were the details. It's something he can do while he's recuperating in bed. I'll be checking out some more technical angles, and you, Lydia, might look into where we stand legally."

"That shouldn't be too difficult to do," she said, going from glass to glass with the pitcher of lemonade. "I know several attorneys downtown who specialize in laws relating to manufacturer liability."

Penny and David looked a little lost, and finally Penny had the courage to admit it. "This may sound dumb, but what laws are we talking about, exactly?"

"It's not dumb at all," Lydia replied with a patient smile. "What we're seeking to know is, if Federal Motors has been producing faulty brakes, are they legally, financially, and morally responsible for the accidents? And what can we the public, or our elected government representatives do to get Federal Motors to meet its responsibilities?"

David shrugged. "It seems pretty clear-cut to me. If Federal made those bad brakes, it's got to pay for damages caused by them."

Lydia shook her finger. "It is more clear-cut today than it ever was before, thanks to men like Ralph Nader, who have been fighting to make manufacturers meet their responsibilities. But not very long ago the manufacturers enjoyed almost unlimited power. For instance, for a long time, the manufacturer of a car was not responsible for something like brake failure. It took a hard-fought legal battle to change this."

"Who had been responsible until then?" David asked, shaking his head in amazement.

"The dealer who sold the car," their friend answered.

"That's ridiculous," David exclaimed.

"Be that as it may, that used to be the law. But even today the matter of liability, or legal and financial responsibility, is far from simple. No large corporation likes to confess it has made a faulty product. It not only hurts the corporation's public image, but costs it tremendous amounts of money. Discovery of a serious manufacturing error in an automobile, to name one example, may mean that tens of thousands of cars must be returned so that the fault can be corrected. You can imagine how expensive that is! So, many companies will fight attempts to prove or publicize the existence of such errors. Some companies have even gone so far as to create false records, or bribe people with damaging information to keep their mouths shut. I am not saying Federal Motors would do such a thing, but I don't want you two to feel you can just walk in there, tell them you believe you know something that is going to cost them several hundred thousand dollars to repair, and expect them to shower you with rose petals."

"We'll have to play it cool," David said to his sister.

She nodded. "We have two tasks ahead of us as I see them. First, we have to find out if Federal Motors is producing faulty brakes. Then, if they are, we have to publicize it."

"Or threaten to," Lydia said. "Sometimes just the threat of contacting the newspapers will force a company to meet its obligations." She looked at her watch. "Time for you kids to go home, isn't it?"

"I'll drive them," Ralph volunteered. "That'll give me a chance to coach them on their visit to Federal Motors."

They rose to their feet, but Penny had one last question. "What about Sam?"

"What about him?" Lydia asked. Then recognition entered her eyes. "You mean, if we do prove the brakes failed, can we get him back his job?"

Penny nodded.

Lydia looked surprisingly pessimistic. "Ordinarily I would say yes. But I've heard some things . . ." Her voice faded.

"About Sam? What sort of things?" David wanted to know.

The attorney held up her hands. "I'd rather not say. They're just rumors and there's no point in spreading them. But if there is any truth to them, Sam might not be fit to drive a school bus anyway."

Penny and David looked at each other, then at Lydia, but could not divine what she was referring to. "Oh, come on, Lydia, you're not going to leave us hanging in mid-air this way," David said in his most engaging voice.

But she was not susceptible to his charm this time. "Sorry, young man. The story is available if you go to the right sources, but you won't hear gossip from *me*. And if I know you two, you'll find the right sources."

They made unhappy faces, then looked at Ralph. But Ralph shook his head and said, "Uh-uh. Don't look at me." He led them out of the house and drove them home.

8
At Federal Motors

The Number 6 bus pulled up to the corner of Muncie Avenue and Warren Street. Pulling their raincoat collars close to their cheeks, David and Penny stepped down onto the wet sidewalk. Luckily it was only about twenty yards across a handsome pink-stoned plaza to the entrance of the Federal Motors building. They made a dash for it, the gusty wind pelting their umbrella with large drops of rain.

Friday was usually a crowded day in New Manchester, but the rain had kept a lot of shoppers home. It had also cleared the air of the usual pall of smog and soot that hung over the city.

Federal Motors' main assembly plant and central offices were located in the Midwest, but because of the volume of business it did on the East Coast the company had a regional office in New Manchester. It was a tall, graceful, impressive building, the most beautiful on the city's skyline, and David and Penny felt awed to have business there.

They paused in front of a directory in the lobby and scanned it until they found *Executive Offices——21.*

"Wow, the top floor of the building!" Penny said. "I'm impressed."

"That's the whole idea," David observed. "Remember what Ralph told us. If we only look at the surface things, we'll be so impressed that we'll come away with a big fat zero on our investigation."

"We can make believe we're impressed," Penny said as they stepped into a sleek, chrome-walled elevator.

"That shouldn't be too difficult," David said, whistling. "It really is quite a place."

The elevator took off like a rocket and came to an abrupt halt at the twenty-first floor. They paused for a second as the door opened, and Penny said, "Wait a moment, I think I left my stomach on the floor."

They stepped out, knees still a little weak from the wild ride, and blinked at the brilliant sweep of space before them. The reception area was as big as a tennis court, with deep, red carpeting from wall to wall. The walls were paneled with dark-grained wood on which hung colorful watercolor paintings of Federal Motors' current line of vehicles—cars, trucks, buses, and farm machinery. Even the tractors looked elegant. A long, curving reception desk stood about twenty paces in front of them, and behind it sat a red-headed woman glamorous enough to be a movie star. To one side of her a switch-

board panel hummed, buzzed, and blinked like the control
board of a spaceship.

The receptionist smiled warmly as they stepped up to the
desk. "May I help you?"

David tried to affect a mature baritone voice, but it croaked
as he said, "We have an appointment with Mr. Austin."

"Your names?"

"David . . . uh, Mr. and Miss Case."

She pressed a button and announced their names. "For a
second I thought you were going to ask for her autograph,"
Penny whispered with a mischievous glint in her eye.

"That's not funny," her brother replied.

The receptionist asked them to wait a moment. Then a
door to their left opened and a tall, handsome, smiling man
strode out to greet them. He introduced himself as Mr. Austin and asked them to come with him. They followed him
through the door and along a chain of white corridors that
had so many pictures of the company's vehicles and automotive products on the walls that it might have been an art gallery. He ushered them into his office, a spacious room whose
far wall was a solid piece of glass with a magnificent view of
New Manchester. "Too bad it's raining," he apologized. "On
a clear day you can see the hills twenty miles away. Would
you like a soft drink?" He went to what appeared to be a
bookshelf, but when he pulled a knob a panel opened up re-
vealing a small refrigerator. Penny and David each accepted
a ginger ale.

"As I understand it from your science teacher, Mr. Carter,
you are here to do research on automotive safety. That's very
laudable. It's a subject that's been very much in the news

lately, and of course we here at Federal Motors are vitally concerned about it. Although we like to think we build beautiful vehicles, we have never sacrificed safety to beauty." His voice was smooth and his manner self-confident, like a TV announcer's. Ralph Carter had told them that instilling trust was the job of the public relations man, and certainly Mr. Austin was very good at his job. But they kept in mind Ralph's final words of advice: "Be skeptical, or you'll end up buying a car from the man."

So although Penny and David nodded agreeably as Mr. Austin spoke, they resisted the temptation to accept everything he told them at face value.

After his introductory speech, he rose and said, "You realize, I'm sure, that this is not a factory, so I can't show you vehicles actually being produced. But we do have scale models of some of our vehicles, illustrations of products, and other exhibits which will give you a good idea of what you might see if you visited our Midwest plant. Come this way."

They followed him down a hallway until they arrived at another office. There they were introduced to a Mr. Marley, who was in charge of exhibits. They summoned a Mr. Cassiday on the telephone, explaining that he was an engineer who could answer any technical questions they might have. After a moment, a young, athletic-looking man looked in and was introduced as Mr. Cassiday. In sharp contrast to the two public relations men in their plain business suits and neatly trimmed hair, Mr. Cassiday wore no tie or jacket and his blond hair was long and rather bushy. David and Penny liked him immediately.

The five took an elevator to the nineteenth floor and stepped out into a dimly lit exhibition hall. David and

Penny's eyes immediately focused on a table in the center of the room on which stood a model of Federal Motors' main assembly plant, a sprawling complex of low buildings. A panel with dozens of buttons on it was attached to the table. Mr. Marley invited the children to press some of them. When they did, various buildings lit up from within so that they could see, in perfect miniature, the activities involved in manufacturing vehicles. Mr. Marley took over the panel and took them on a brief, imaginary tour of the factory, demonstrating how motor vehicles are assembled, from the arrival of parts made in smaller plants around the country, to the loading of finished cars, buses, trucks, and other vehicles onto trains destined for every corner of the United States and ports to carry them overseas. For a grand finale, he threw a couple of switches which lit up the entire plant and started assembly lines moving, so that the whole process could be seen at once. David and Penny gasped and murmured. It was a splendid sight. There was even a model car racing around the test track outside the factory.

Mr. Marley then led them to an exhibition of photographs portraying the history of Federal Motors. The collection was extensive and he touched only on the highlights. He spoke without much expression, suggesting he had been through his speech many, many times.

Although this too was interesting to the Cases, they began to grow impatient to take up the question of safety, which was the purpose of their visit. Young Mr. Cassiday seemed to sense their unrest and flashed knowing looks at them while Mr. Marley spoke about Federal Motors' role during World War II, manufacturing tanks and other armored vehicles.

They came to the end of the photo exhibition and passed

through an archway into a tremendous hall. "Ah, I think this is what we're looking for," David said under his breath. The room was filled with pedestals on which reposed, like statues, models of automotive components and systems. Many were made of transparent plastic, and some of the metal ones had their outer skins partially cut away, exposing the working parts inside. Here was an automobile engine made of Lucite, with every part working perfectly. Here was a cutaway model of a differential, showing how a system of gears conveys energy from the drive shaft to the rear wheels. Here was a complete electrical system so complex that the wires comprising it formed the shape of a car, the way a model of a human circulatory system takes the shape of a person.

Suspended from the ceiling were other exhibits: a giant spark plug whose tip flashed bright red; a stick shift which moved automatically from neutral position to first, second, third gear and reverse; a steering wheel which turned back and forth demonstrating how a car's wheels are swung left or right. David and Penny had briefly studied the mechanics of the automobile in Ralph Carter's science class, but only now did the two-dimensional diagrams in their school books come vividly to life. It was difficult for them to keep their minds on their mission with these dazzling displays beckoning them to study the marvels of modern technology.

Nevertheless, they kept their eyes out for the one display they had really come to see. Penny spied it first and nudged her brother. On a pedestal at the far end of the hall was a model of a brake system. A brake pedal moved in an out, increasing and releasing the pressure of hydraulic fluid through tubes leading to the wheels of the vehicle. Inside each wheel was a small cylinder with pistons linked to the braking mech-

anism. When the brake pedal was depressed by a driver's foot, the increased pressure of the fluid caused brake "shoes" to be pushed against the inside of the brake drum. The resulting friction thus slowed the wheels and brought the vehicle to a halt.

David and Penny drifted casually toward the exhibit, stopping along the way to study several others. When they finally arrived at the brake model, Penny took a small notebook out of her purse and began sketching furiously. David scrutinized every detail, trying to commit it all to memory.

Mr. Austin stood behind them for a minute and then said, "Ah yes, I'd almost forgotten. You're particularly interested in safety aspects. I'll turn you over to Mr. Cassiday, our engineer. He knows cars so well he could put one together by himself in the dark."

"Not really," he laughed, "but I did disassemble one in the dark once in three seconds flat."

Penny stared. "How did you do that?"

"I skidded into a tree," he replied with a chuckle. "As a matter of fact, that's how I came to specialize in safety. After my accident I went back to the spot, a sharp curve where I learned a lot of other cars had skidded out of control on rainy days. I persuaded the town's highway engineers to cut grooves into that stretch, running parallel with the direction of travel. Tires grip those grooves much better than they do the flat pavement, and I'm happy to say there hasn't been an accident on that stretch since then."

"What a great idea," David said with admiration.

"Oh, there are lots of good ideas, but you have to fight to get them adopted. Some government agencies and big corporations are slow to act on them. It costs money, you know."

Mr. Marley frowned at the outspoken engineer, but Mr. Austin quickly smiled at David and Penny and said, "That's why we've been hiring young men like Mr. Cassiday. They have fresh ideas and they're impatient to put them into practice. They keep us older executives from getting too stodgy. On the other hand, they don't always understand the economics of the auto industry. Why, we could probably build 100 per cent safe cars tomorrow, but they'd be so expensive that we would go out of business. So we sometimes have to make compromises."

"Compromises," Mr. Cassiday repeated with a tone of distaste. This dialogue did not contribute directly to the Cases' investigation, but it gave them a fascinating insight into corporate policies that might set the stage for the production of inferior parts. Was the failure of Sam Gilman's brakes the result of some compromise between safety and cost, they wondered?

"I gather that brakes interest you particularly," Mr. Cassiday said.

David turned to him. "Yes, that's our research assignment: to learn all about brakes. Tell me, is the same type of brake used in cars, trucks, and buses?"

"The principles are the same, but obviously we wouldn't use the same brake in a ten-ton truck that we use in a one-ton car."

"Do you have a model of the kind of brakes you'd use in a truck—or a bus?" David asked a bit nervously.

"No, but we have diagrams somewhere on file. Unfortunately, I won't be able to show them to you because they're supposed to be kept secret. We don't want our competitors to steal our technical information." Penny and David looked disappointed, and Mr. Cassiday said, "I suppose there'd be no harm in giving you a rough sketch or two of the differences." He looked at the public relations men and they shrugged indifferently. He took Penny's pad and pencil and quickly diagrammed a variety of brake components, chatting amiably about what he was doing. "The essential difference between a car's brakes and the braking system we use on buses or trucks, aside from size and weight, lies in the construction of the hydraulic fluid master cylinder," and he proceeded to explain how that component varied from the one used in an automobile. Penny and David did their best to follow his explanation, and he had a gift for reducing difficult technical concepts to simple, clear pictures. Still, they did not grasp everything he told them, and they wished Vernon were here, for he would not only know what questions to ask, but what the answers meant as well.

When he was finished, David asked him, "Can brakes fail?"

"Sure. Anything made by humans can fail. If brakes are made well, however, the odds against failure are extremely high."

"How might brakes fail?" Penny asked.

"A number of ways. There might be a leak in the hydraulic system. The brake shoes might become so worn as to lose their grip on the brake drums. A valve might slip or become stuck."

"Is it possible for a brake to work perfectly one time, fail the next, and work perfectly the time after that?"

"Strange question," Mr. Cassiday remarked, searching the ceiling absently for an answer. "Why do you ask?"

"Oh, I don't know," David said, trying not to state his suspicions too bluntly. "I guess I was thinking of the bus accident that happened in our town a few weeks ago."

The two public relations men looked at him. "Which accident was that?" Mr. Austin said.

David reviewed it briefly.

Mr. Austin still looked puzzled but Mr. Marley said, "Ah, yes, I remember reading about it in the papers. The driver said the brakes failed, but subsequent tests proved he was lying just to cover up his reckless driving."

"But could it happen the way he said it did, just for the sake of argument?" David persisted.

"Absolutely not," Mr. Marley snapped back without hesitation.

"Not a chance," Mr. Austin concurred.

They turned to Mr. Cassiday for confirmation, but his eyes were still wandering around the ceiling, as if the answer might be suspended from it like one of the exhibits.

"What about it, Mr. Cassiday? Do you agree with them?" Penny said.

"My father has a proverb," the engineer replied. " 'Never say never.' I admit the event is highly improbable, but I wouldn't say it could never happen. Under certain special conditions, it could occur. The brake design is, after all, a fairly new one. But I agree with my colleagues. It's far more probable that the bus driver drove carelessly."

"Just one more question," David said, looking uneasily at the public relations men. "Under what 'special conditions' might that bus's brakes work, fail, then work again?"

"Gee," Mr. Cassiday said, "I'd have to look into that thoroughly. I can't give you an offhand reply. But I'll tell you what I'll do. I'll fool around with the idea if I have any spare time."

"And let us know?" said Penny, scribbling their phone

number on a piece of paper and handing it to him.

"Sure," he said with a friendly grin.

"Well," Mr. Austin said to David and Penny, "we stand corrected by Mr. Cassiday. We won't say it could never happen. But I'll tell you kids that the chances of its happening are so slim as to be next to impossible. And I'll stake my thirty-five years of experience in the automotive industry on that statement."

"Add my twenty-nine years," Mr. Marley added.

"I'm afraid I can only offer five," Mr. Cassiday said with a shrug.

"And all this time I thought you were born yesterday," Mr. Austin said with a good-natured laugh.

Mr. Cassiday flushed and joined in the laughter. Although there was clearly a conflict between them, it was more a friendly rivalry than real hostility.

The three walked Penny and David to the elevator and bade them good-bye cordially.

"Do you suppose they're hiding something?" Penny asked David as the elevator plummeted to the ground floor.

Her brother shook his head. "No, I think they're just proud men who can't believe their company can make the sort of mistake we were talking about."

"And do you know something? They may be right."

"Never say never," David reminded his sister as they emerged onto the rain-slick plaza of the Federal Motors building.

9
The Revolt of the Machines

Every now and then in everybody's life comes a day when nothing goes right. By ten o'clock the following Monday morning, Vernon Stevenson began to suspect that day had come for him. By eleven he was convinced of it.

It had started with breakfast, when Nurse Minster brought him someone else's meal by mistake. That someone else must have been pretty ill, for the breakfast consisted of a bowl of sugarless, saltless, milkless oatmeal and a slice of butterless, jellyless toast. Vernon began to get ill just looking at it. The nurse finally corrected the error, but it had set the tone for the rest of the day's events, the next being what Vernon termed The Revolt of the Machines.

Although he could create sophisticated machines out of

commonplace materials—his ingenuity was the talk of the hospital—Vernon had not yet quite mastered the knack of building his machines to last. But why they should all fail within ten minutes of one another he couldn't understand.

The first to malfunction was the device for raising his bed to a sitting position. It had worked at breakfast time, and again when he lowered it for an hour's nap. And it worked when he awoke—worked and worked and worked, going from the prone position to a sitting position to a folding position! Vernon found himself being bent over double like a letter about to be sealed in an envelope. Luckily, just as his nose was approaching his knees, a wire under the bed snapped. He managed with considerable difficulty to remove his broken leg from the traction system that suspended it at the end of the bed and crawl out of the trap before the air permanently left his lungs.

After cranking the bed by hand to a sitting position, he climbed back in and decided to get down to work on the problem of the bus brakes. David and Penny had visited him over the weekend, told him all about their visit to Federal Motors, and given him sketches and verbal accounts of the brake systems as explained by Mr. Cassiday. He had spent Sunday evening studying the information and trying to figure out how the system might fail. He had come up with a number of possibilities, but his theories kept collapsing around one key fact: that after failing, the brakes had worked again.

Now, settled comfortably after his scary experience with the bed, he tugged on the cord attached to the shopping bag containing his books and papers, which was parked in a corner. The heavy freight slid halfway up the wire, shuddered, and spilled through a tear in the bag, dumping the books and papers all over the floor. Vernon laboriously climbed out of bed, picked up the books—no small accomplishment with one leg rigidly encased in plaster—and retired to bed again, panting.

The final indignity came when the phone rang. He reached above his head and pulled the cord to bring it to him. The tray caught on the lamp, then sprang free and swept toward his head like a heavy trapeze. He ducked out of the way just in time. The tray swung past him and hurled the phone on the floor with a clatter.

Trembling, he hauled in the phone by its wire and put the receiver to his ear. "Vernon? Vernon? What's going on there? Are you all right?" It was his mother.

"Yes," he said in a shaky voice, "I'm all right."

"What was all that racket? My ears are ringing."

"Nothing, really. It's just that I'm beginning to think I'm the target of an assassination plot."

"What are you talking about?"

"The machines are after me," he said.

There was a long, troubled pause at the other end of the wire. Vernon realized what must be running through his mother's mind: that the brain damage everyone had feared was beginning to manifest itself in the form of hallucinations. He quickly explained what had been happening to him all morning long, and his mother hung up, relieved that her son had not lost his wits.

Resolving to have as little as possible to do with machines for the rest of the day, he took up his work on the brake problem in earnest, but after an hour of concentrated study he threw his papers down in disgust. He looked at his watch. It was eleven, and the mail was supposed to be delivered at ten thirty.

After conferring with David, Penny, Ralph, and Lydia the previous week, Vernon had agreed to write to the State Motor Vehicle Bureau, as well as to those of a dozen other states, inquiring about recent school-bus accidents. By now he should have had at least a couple of replies, and he was particularly interested in the one from his own state. That one would tell him whether any similarities had been discovered between the Aubrey Park accident and the one in Verona. Where was the mail anyway?

He reached for the buzzer to summon Nurse Minster, hesitated a moment as he remembered that today was the day for The Revolt of the Machines, then took a chance and pressed the button. Miraculously, it worked, and Nurse Minster stuck her head in the door a few moments later.

"Is the mail in?"

"Yes. Are you expecting notification of the Nobel Prize for science?" she said with a throaty laugh at her own sense of humor.

"No, but what I'm expecting is almost as important to me."

She held her hands out and shrugged. "I'm sorry, but there was nothing for you. I'll bring it to you first thing tomorrow if you do get any." She smiled warmly and seemed to be feeling guilty about teasing Vernon. She liked to pretend to be tough and stern, but she betrayed an obvious affection for children, especially boys, being the mother of four of them. She patted him gently on the shoulder, smoothed out his sheets and plumped up his pillow, and left.

Vernon lay in bed growing more and more depressed. Nothing seemed to be going right today, and suddenly things that had not bothered him before began to get him down. He had managed to make the most of his essentially uninteresting hospital environment and had had no shortage of visitors. But now he began to feel homesick and lonely. He was impatient to be released from the hospital, to sleep in his own bed again and return to the dozen projects that lay unfinished on the work table in his basement, to eat something other than hospital food, to ride around the neighborhood on bikes with his friends. He felt tears brimming in his eyes.

Then he pulled himself up straight. "This is ridiculous!" he said out loud. He dabbed his eyes, took a deep breath, and plunged into action to cure the funk that had been creeping over him like deadly quicksand.

He reached—cautiously this time—for the cord over his head and pulled the telephone over. There were no phone books in the room, so he dialed the information operator and got the number of the State Motor Vehicle Bureau. He dialed it. The switchboard operator at the bureau asked him what he wanted. Vernon explained the complicated matter as well as he could, but the woman misunderstood him and, believing he wished to report an accident, connected him with the wrong department. When the man on the other end of the line realized the error, he signaled the operator and told her to connect Vernon with a Mr. Jordan. Thinking the man had said Gordon, she connected Vernon with a person who thought Vernon was applying for a chauffeur's license. Mr. Gordon buzzed the operator after realizing he was the wrong man. She then connected Vernon with Mr. Jordan's secretary, who said Mr. Jordan was out of the office but would Mr. Poole do.

By this time Vernon had been on the telephone for what seemed like hours and had begun to get the feeling he was going to spend the rest of the week bouncing around from one wrong official to another. Wearily he said, "Yes, I suppose so."

Fortunately, Mr. Poole was friendly, interested in Vernon's story, and eager to cooperate. "It sounds to me as if you may be onto something genuinely important," he said.

"I'm glad you think so. Everyone else down there treated me as if I threatened to infect them with a disease."

"That's the bureaucratic mentality," Mr. Poole laughed.

"What's that?"

"Bureaucrats are minor government officials," he explained. "Some of them don't care for responsibility and try to limit their tasks to the simplest problems, such as filling out printed forms. If you bring them a problem that requires using their intelligence, they get annoyed and try to pass you along to somebody else. Of course, there are many responsible people working in government bureaus; I guess you just got a run of the poorer kinds."

"I'm sure glad I got *you*." Vernon sighed.

Mr. Poole laughed. "Actually, your problem doesn't fall strictly within my range of responsibilities either, but sometimes a man has to do other people's work for them if he wants to accomplish anything important. So I'll be glad to follow up on this matter for you."

Vernon thanked him profusely and hung up, feeling he'd made progress for the first time that day.

While he was on the telephone, an orderly had come into his room and straightened it up, dumping the contents of the wastebasket into a large refuse container, mopping the floor, and cleaning the toilet and sink. Vernon could hear the man muttering in the bathroom about something. Just as he hung up the phone, he saw the orderly throw a rag angrily on the floor and storm out of the room. After a few minutes he returned with Nurse Minster and showed her something in the bathroom. They kept turning the taps on the sink on and off and conferring about some sort of difficulty. Nurse Minster finally said, "Well, how should I know? I'm a nurse, not a plumber," and came out of the bathroom shaking her head.

"What's the problem?" Vernon asked.

"Oh, nothing really. There's a rubber stopper in your sink that won't stay in the hole. Teddy here thinks I have nothing more important to do than worry about it."

"That's funny," Vernon said, tilting his head thoughtfully. "When I run water in that sink the stopper stays in the hole."

"You can see for yourself," Teddy said.

Vernon, who was now allowed out of bed to walk around with the aid of crutches or ride down the hall in his wheelchair for short periods of time, climbed out of the covers and limped to the bathroom. The orderly took the flat rubber stopper in hand and pressed it over the hole in the sink, but sure enough it slipped off. Vernon tried it, taking care to apply pressure evenly so that one edge didn't slip away while another edge was being held on. Yet the stopper refused to stay put. "Why should that happen?" he said aloud.

"Well, you apply your sublime genius to the problem,"

Nurse Minster said. "I can't be bothered. I have human lives to attend to."

"Frankly, neither can I," Vernon said, and shrugged apologetically at the orderly. "I have human lives to attend to, too." He struggled back into bed and tackled his diagrams of the bus brakes with renewed determination.

After a half hour he heard the rattling of dishes and realized the lunch cart was approaching. He got out of bed and went into the bathroom to wash up. He placed the rubber stopper over the hole, filled the sink with water, and washed his hands. Then, as he was drying them on a towel, he realized what had just happened. "The stopper works!" He went back to the sink and tried to put the stopper on the hole. "Now it doesn't work! This is crazy."

Of course, nothing was really crazy to Vernon. He believed that everything had a basis in fact or logic, and if something behaved "crazily" it was only because he hadn't figured out what all the facts were or what was the logic behind them.

Now his curiosity was stimulated to the point where he would not drop the problem until he'd solved it. He picked up the stopper and examined it closely. It glistened with water. He tried it on the hole. It slipped off because it was wet. Of course! The stopper worked when it was dry; when wet, it failed. The riddle was explained. It was easy once you applied common sense to a problem. He resolved to get hold of the orderly after lunch and explain how he had solved the mystery of the on-again–off-again stopper.

Nurse Minster came into the room pushing a tall wagon on which about a dozen trays were stacked. "I've got the right meal for you this time," she said, setting a tray before him and lifting the cover off the plate. It was a delicious luncheon of roast beef, potatoes, vegetables, a salad, roll and butter, dessert, and milk.

Vernon consumed it greedily. This had been the most trying day he'd had since arriving in the hospital, and he'd worked up a ferocious appetite. The revolt of his machines, the frustrating challenge of the bus brakes, his momentary depression, the tedious delays on the phone—why, he was hungry enough to eat a second meal just like the first. And the worst part of it was, the only thing he had to show for all his emotional ups and downs was his insignificant victory over the sink stopper.

It was not until he was draining his glass of milk that it dawned on him that the sink stopper might not be so insignificant. In fact, possibly it was the most important thing that had happened to him in weeks. "Good Lord, I think that's the answer!" He grabbed his books and papers and diagrams and studied the bus brakes again. He tapped Mr. Cassiday's sketch with his index finger. "There it is; there's the villain." He threw the covers off, clambered down, and limped to his wheelchair. He plopped heavily into it, then reached underneath the footrest, searching for the swtich.

Among the numerous gadgets Vernon had had David bring to the hospital was a large battery and a small but powerful electric motor. After his first trip down the halls in a wheelchair Vernon's arms ached, so he had decided to motorize it. After thinking about it for a while he chose a simple friction drive similar to those he had seen on motorbikes. It had proven more difficult than he'd anticipated, especially because the work had to be done in semi-darkness when the nurse thought he was asleep. He had not had an opportunity to try the machine out since completing it, but now he wanted to get to Sam Gilman's room down the hall as fast as possible to tell him about his exciting discovery.

He found the switch. The little motor hummed and suddenly the chair lurched forward with such force that it threw Vernon's head back. It took off through the open door of his room and into the busy corridor. Wheelchairs are steered by applying pressure to either the left wheel or the right, and Vernon placed his right hand on the right wheel to make the chair turn right. It did, but the vehicle was moving so fast that the spinning rubber burned his palm.

In an instant he realized he had made several mistakes in designing his motorized wheelchair. It had no speed control, just On and Off. When on, the motor propelled him at about ten miles an hour, which in a crowded hospital corridor is an insane speed. It had no steering wheel, and, as he had just learned, it was impossible to turn the wheels by hand without getting a bad burn. The only way to stop the machine was to reach under the footrest and turn the motor off, but that was hard to do with a cast-stiffened leg, and besides, it was all he could do to keep from running people down, crashing into the wall, or ramming other wheelchairs.

"Watch out! Watch out!" he cried, bearing down on two nurses' aides. They leaped out of the way only to reveal another obstacle right in front of them, an orderly's cart. Vernon hit the left wheel, stinging his hand but swerving just in time. But he struck the wall, bounced off it, struck the opposite wall, then jolted forward again in the direction of—Nurse Minster. The stout woman's mouth opened in disbelief as

she stumbled out of his way. "Vernon, are you out of your mind?"

"Can't stop!" he shouted back. He caught a glimpse of the number 354 on a door behind her. Sam's room was 356. Just as he was passing it, he jammed the heel of his hand against the wheel. The chair made a sharp turn, rammed the half-open door, and bounced into the room. It slammed against the bed and came to a halt. The engine was still running, however, and as the wheels tried to turn it got hotter and hotter and began to smoke. Vernon felt for the switch but couldn't find it. Crackling sounds and blue sparks were coming from under his seat, and the room was filling with acrid smoke.

Luckily, Nurse Minster ran into the room, reached under the chair, and yanked a handful of wires out of the engine. "Young man," she announced between heavy puffs of breath, "your automotive days are over."

Vernon was too frightened and ashamed to look up for several moments. When he finally did he got yet another shock. The occupant of the bed was not Sam Gilman, but an old lady Vernon had never seen before. Her eyes were saucer-shaped with terror and her trembling hands shielded her eyes as if a tank had rolled into her room and was about to open fire.

"But . . . where's Sam?"

"He was released three days ago," Nurse Minster said, throwing open the windows to let the smoke out. A crowd of patients and hospital personnel were pressed around the doorway to see what had happened.

Vernon hung his head. "Tell me, Nurse Minster, do you believe in horoscopes?"

"No," she said brusquely. "Why?"

"Because I believe I should have read mine before I began this day. I'm sure it said I should do nothing but sleep."

"Whatever it said, I'm going to see to it that you sleep the rest of the day," she said in a no-nonsense voice as she pushed his wheelchair out the door.

10
Discouraging Odds

"Will you *please* tell us what's so funny?"

Penny addressed the question to her brother, who was clutching the phone and rolling around the floor of the Cases' den wheezing with laughter. Mr. and Mrs. Case stood behind Penny, staring at their son. It was maddening to see someone laughing hysterically and not know to whom he was speaking and what the joke was. Tears streaming down his cheeks, David could only shake his head at his sister.

"And then you . . . you rammed into Sam's bed? You almost set it . . . on fire? What did The Monster do? I'll bet she was! You're lucky she didn't wrap it around your head. What did Sam say? He wasn't? A little old lady! Where was Sam? Uh-huh. No, I don't know. But you still haven't told me what the sink stopper has to do with the bus accident."

At last the laughter faded and David became serious. For several minutes he simply nodded and grunted, "Uh-huh, uh-huh, uh-huh." Mr. and Mrs. Case shrugged and left the room, but Penny stayed behind trying to figure out what the "uh-huhs" referred to. By this time she'd deduced that the party at the other end of the line was Vernon, but everything else in David's dialogue remained a mystery.

And when David cried out, "I see! Of course! Vernon, I think you've got it!" Penny could scarcely contain herself. She paced around the den pleading silently with her brother to get off the phone so that he could tell her what the call was all about.

At long last, saying, "I'll try to find him," David put the phone back on its cradle. The instant he did, Penny inundated him with questions, and even his parents materialized out of nowhere as if they'd been waiting just out of range for David to finish his call.

Savoring the pleasure of knowing something they didn't know, David very slowly recounted his conversation with Vernon, starting with the story of the runaway wheelchair. His parents and sister laughed heartily, but not as heartily as David had, for they knew he was holding back a very important piece of information.

"But what about Sam's brakes?" Mr. Case asked impatiently. "You said that the reason Vernon got in his wheelchair and went to find Sam was to tell him he'd figured out how the brakes failed."

"I was coming to that. It dawned on Vernon after he'd helped an orderly figure out why a rubber stopper stayed over its hole in the sink on one occasion, slipped off the next, and stayed put the one after that. The answer is, if the stopper is dry, it will stick; if it's wet, it won't."

"But I still don't see what that has to do with brakes," Mrs. Case said. She looked around at her husband and daughter, who were just as much in the dark as she was.

"Well," David replied, "as Vernon explained it to me, there is a critical seal in the master cylinder of the braking system used on this particular type of bus. This seal will work properly only if it remains perfectly dry. But if something happened to make it wet, it might leak when Sam stepped on the brakes. Then the brake fluid could be forced back into the master cylinder instead of out to the wheel cylinders when the brakes are applied."

Penny and Mrs. Case nodded agreement, but the look in their eyes indicated that they didn't quite follow the principles and were taking David's word for it. But Mr. Case, trained in engineering, had a light of recognition in his eyes. He turned to his wife and daughter. "You see, in order for brakes to function it is necessary to develop pressure in the brake fluid. Under normal circumstances the fluid cannot escape from the system, and the pressure is produced whenever the brake pedal is depressed. But if there were a leak in the system, the fluid would instead be bypassed through the leak, and it would not be possible to develop the hydraulic pressure required to activate the wheel cylinders." This time Penny and Mrs. Case followed the logic of it. Mr. Case turned back to David with another question. "Why would that seal be wet one time and dry the next?"

"Vernon doesn't know himself. He says only close examination of the seal will give us the answer. But his guess is that there is a weakness or flaw in the master cylinder which will allow the fluid to flow in under very special circumstances. That would make the seal wet. Then the fluid could flow out through that same flaw. The seal would soon become dry, and unless the circumstances were duplicated perfectly on another occasion, that seal might function correctly forever after."

"What special circumstances might activate this flaw, do you suppose?" Mr. Case pursued, his interest growing intense. "After all, I did try to duplicate the conditions that led to the accident."

"You may not have been able to duplicate them precisely enough," his son replied. "Maybe the air temperature was a factor. Maybe the wheels hit a certain bump when Sam was driving, but you missed it when you took the bus down the hill. Maybe Sam pumped the brakes a certain number of times. Maybe—and this is Vernon's guess—it was a combination of all those factors, a combination so special that it could be repeated only by sheer luck."

"It would require elaborate inspection and testing procedures to determine whether Vernon is right or not."

"Yes, and only Federal Motors has the facilities for that," said David.

"Why can't you get Federal Motors to undertake the job?" Mrs. Case asked.

Penny had the answer to that one. "If you'd been there with us the day we visited their offices, you'd know why. They're convinced it's impossible for their brakes to fail that way. It's far easier for them to believe Sam was the cause of the failure."

Mr. Case turned his eyes away from his children. "I'm afraid it was easier for a lot of people to blame Sam."

The four lapsed into silence. It was broken by Mrs. Case, who echoed what was in all their minds. "Well, there's no sense in crying over spilled milk. You've got to bring this to the attention of those who are in a position to check out your speculations. And if your speculations are right, then you've got to take action to have all the school buses using that brake system examined and repaired. And of course, you'll have to try to get Sam's job back for him."

"That's a tall order," Mr. Case said to his wife. "It means confronting Federal Motors, government officials, and a lot of other people with what is still an unproven theory. And I can tell you from experience how difficult it is to budge big corporations and government agencies. Unless we have overwhelming proof, and unless we publicize it, they will remain indifferent to our appeals. They will tell us it costs too much money, or too much time and labor, to investigate a claim based on practically no sound evidence whatsoever. They will tell us the odds against our being right are a million to one. And I have to admit there's sense in that position. I myself am by no means convinced your theory has a sound basis in fact. What it boils down to, then, is that you two kids have more homework to do."

"Yes," Penny said with a discouraged air, "but just what *can* we do?"

"There are two areas you can work in," her father said. "The first is to secure more proof for your theory. The second is to try to bring to the public's attention that there may have been a flaw in the brake system of Sam's bus. I have some ideas on both scores that you might try following up. And I'll be more than glad to help in whatever ways I can."

"But even you agree that the odds against us are a million to one," David protested.

"Yes," Mr. Case said, "but with the lives of countless children possibly depending on this, I consider it a worthwhile gamble."

11
Ken Sims Explains

The Veterans of Foreign Wars Lodge was a simple, two-story red brick structure located a short distance from the elevated highway that separated the part of Aubrey Park they lived in from the poor, run-down neighborhood known as the Viaduct. David and Penny took a Number 4 bus the following day, got off at the last stop before the Viaduct, and walked back two blocks. Although they were still in Aubrey Park, this part of it was not as pleasant as the section in which they lived. It was as if the decay and poverty of the Viaduct had seeped across the highway and blighted some of the other side.

"What exactly is the Veterans of Foreign Wars?" Penny asked her brother as they ascended the chipped concrete stairs leading to the building's entrance.

"It's an organization for servicemen or former servicemen who have fought overseas," he said. "They hold social functions here, such as reunions for men who belonged to the same fighting units. They also perform services for members, like making sure that veterans receive any benefits they're entitled to."

"So Sam is a veteran?"

"I guess so. World War II, I'd imagine."

"I wonder if he was a hero."

"Ralph Carter says if you can just survive a war, you're a hero."

They passed through the doors and into a lobby containing a fascinating array of displays. Before going to look for Sam they strolled around the circular gallery examining some of them. On the walls were dramatic murals of famous battles, banners belonging to various regiments, and brass plaques listing men from the community who had died in combat. There were large glass cabinets containing souvenirs of war: Japanese swords, German helmets, Italian rifles, and arms from Russia, China, and even North Korea and Vietnam. The display of medals and ribbons was so interesting they wanted to linger over it longer, but David reminded his sister they had business to attend to.

They crossed the floor to a desk, behind which sat a very old man with thin white hair and tired eyes who looked like he might be a veteran of the Civil War. "Do you know where we might find Sam Gilman?" David asked him.

He immediately pointed to a door marked *Lounge*. "You'll find him in there, sitting at a corner table with Ken Sims."

They thanked him and followed his quivering finger through an oak door and into a smoky room with a bar and a number of tables. Men in groups of three and four sat around the tables drinking, and from their gestures and snatches of conversation, David and Penny realized they were talking about their wartime adventures.

As the ancient soldier had said, Sam was sitting in a corner with a chubby man they assumed was Ken Sims. Unlike the rest of the men, Sam and his friend were not engaged in animated discussion, but stared glumly at one another.

"Hello, Sam." David smiled.

Sam peered blankly at the children. It took several seconds for him to recognize them. Then he said, "Hey, it's the Case kids!" He started to grin, but his mouth froze midway, as if remembering that he was not supposed to be happy. Furrowing his brows, he said, "How did you know I was here?"

"We got your home address and phone number from the hospital. We called you and got your landlady or neighbor or something. She said you would probably be here. How do you feel, Sam?"

He turned slightly to reveal his arm still in a sling. "Oh, it's coming along all right." He looked somewhat embarrassed and filled the uncomfortable gap with, "This is an old friend of mine, Ken Sims. We fought in France together in World War II. He saved my life."

Ken Sims waved his hand modestly. "Aw, come on, Sam, you saved mine."

"We saved each other's, I guess," Sam said.

Ken Sims looked up at the kids. "Case . . . Say, wasn't that your father who testified at Sam's hearing about the brakes?"

"Yes," David said, "and that's what we're here—"

"I liked him," Sims said. "He struck me as a fair man. He bent over backward to give Sam the benefit of the doubt. It was that Mrs. Parsons I didn't like. She just wanted to hurt Sam."

"Say, just what do you kids want?" Sam demanded.

"We want to talk to you about the accident," Penny said.

"What about it? It's all been decided. Your father and the rest of them have seen to that, haven't they?"

"There's some new evidence. Not a lot of it, but enough to make us feel the board may have acted too hastily. Even our father thinks so."

"What kind of evidence?"

"For one thing," said Penny, "we believe we may have spotted a manufacturing flaw in the brake system."

"And for another," said David, "we've learned of another bus accident, one similar to yours. It may have been caused by the same flaw."

"May have," Sam said, dully. "That's not good enough. All you have is a guess and my word for it. Unless you've got real evidence, it's not worth a plugged nickel."

"It is to us," Penny said. "It's worth enough for us to be putting a lot of hard work into getting to the bottom of it."

"Why are you going to so much trouble for my sake?"

"Because you're our friend, Sam. We don't think you got a fair deal. But we're also concerned about all the children riding around in school buses that may be unsafe. If you don't put up a fight against dismissal, this question of faulty brakes will be dropped and no one will hear of it again," said Penny.

"At least not until there's an accident that kills twenty or thirty kids," David amended.

Sam's features softened into that old look of concern for children. Then they hardened again. "So you want me to try to get my job back?"

"Yes," said David. "It would accomplish two things: correcting the injustice that's been done to you, and airing the issue of the brakes."

The bus driver reflected on the proposition, hesitated, then shook his head. "No. No, I'm sorry. If we had a stronger case, I'd say O.K., but with only your 'may haves,' I'd do nothing but humiliate myself the way I did before that hearing. And believe me, that's something I'll never go through again. If you could have seen those faces . . ."

"My father wasn't against you," Penny snapped. "As a matter of fact, it broke his heart to vote to dismiss you, but he didn't think the evidence left him any choice."

"I'm sorry, Penny. I didn't mean anything personal against your father," Sam said. "But everyone there seemed to think the worst of me in spite of all my years of service and my safety record and my reputation with the kids. Why, when that Parsons woman came out with that slander about my private life—"

"But Sam," Ken Sims said, "you didn't do anything to defend yourself against it."

"I wasn't going to bare my soul in front of that woman . . . oh, what does it matter now! The point is, I won't go through that again. I'd rather be out of a job. I'm sorry, kids. It was darned nice of you to come looking for me like this, but . . . I'm sorry." He rose and shuffled out of the room.

Penny, David, and Ken Sims sat mutely facing each other, waiting for someone to break the gloomy silence. At length Sims said, "Can I get you kids a Coke or something? I want to show my appreciation for what you tried to do for Sam."

They let him treat them to lemonades, and upon finishing

his in three gulps, David said, "You were with Sam during the hearing?"

"Yes. It was terrible what happened to Sam."

"I know. I've never seen him so unhappy. But I wonder if you'd mind telling us one thing. Our father wouldn't discuss it with us and everyone else, including Sam, is just as reluctant to talk about it."

Ken Sims was one step ahead of David. "You want to know what Mrs. Parsons said about Sam at the hearing."

"Yes. She obviously used some awful piece of information to clinch her argument that Sam was negligent. If we don't know what she said and how much truth there is in it, how are we going to be able to go on fighting for Sam?"

The round-faced man shifted his glass nervously from hand to hand. "I don't know if Sam would want me to go into it. It's very personal."

Penny looked at David and sighed. "It looks like the biggest obstacle preventing us from helping Sam is Sam himself."

"He's suffered enough," Sims said.

"He may have far more suffering ahead of him than he has behind him," Penny said.

"What do you mean?"

"I mean that if there is a fatal school-bus accident one of these days, Sam will never forgive himself for refusing to fight back."

Penny's argument seemed to make a deep impression on Sam's friend. He puckered his mouth thoughtfully, and appeared on the edge of cooperating with them. David managed to push him across the line with, "If Mrs. Parsons told a lie that day, then Sam has nothing to hide, right?"

"Well, son, it's a little more complicated than that. She

didn't tell a lie so much as a half-truth. She said that Sam was in the care of a psychiatrist."

"A psychiatrist!" David exclaimed. "You mean she accused Sam of being mentally . . . mentally . . ." He could not bring himself to say "ill."

"Unstable?" Penny came to her brother's rescue.

Ken Sims got to his feet. "Listen, kids, I'm not sure you're supposed to be sitting in here. Why don't we go outside and I'll tell you all about it."

"Fine," said Penny. "My eyes are beginning to smart from all this smoke anyway."

They got up and went into the lobby. Sims paused in front of a green regimental flag. "That was our outfit," he said wistfully. "You wouldn't think, to look at me, that I was a tough, trim soldier thirty years ago. And you wouldn't think, to see the way Sam is acting, that he'd run through a hail of bullets to pull a wounded buddy back into a foxhole. It's a funny thing, but most people can endure physical pain better than mental pain. What we're up against with Sam is, he's lost his confidence. He's been wounded emotionally and now he's scared to stick his head out of the foxhole."

They walked out of the building and sat down on the concrete steps. Sims turned his face toward the sun and closed his eyes. "Sam wasn't always a bus driver," he began slowly. "When he came back from the war he went into business for himself, a trucking company. He did real well and had a small fleet of trucks. He decided he needed a partner and took one in, I don't remember the man's name. Unfortunately, the man was crooked and embezzled the company's funds. By the time Sam discovered he was being cheated, the man had left the country and Sam was bankrupt.

"But before the discovery, at the time things were going well for him, Sam married this girl, Martha. I'm afraid she wasn't a very nice woman. She liked money too much. As long as Sam was making a lot of it, she was happy. But when he went broke, she turned sour. She stayed with him but never forgave him. Hardly a day went by in twenty-five years of marriage that she didn't call him a fool—or worse."

"Why did he stay with her?" asked Penny.

Sims shrugged. "These things happen. Habit, I suppose. And guilt—he felt he'd let her down and didn't want to make it worse by leaving her. Maybe hope had something to do with it. He figured that one day he'd find that crook and get his money back, or maybe go into business again and make another fortune. And of course, he still loved her, in spite of all the terrible things she said and did to him. Anyway, that was the story of their life, at least until last year. She finally got fed up and asked him for a divorce. He begged her to reconsider and persuaded her to go with him to a marriage counselor. She agreed and they went to one for a year or so, but it didn't do any good. She divorced him a few months ago, about two months before the accident."

"But where does the psychiatrist . . ." Penny asked.

"That was the marriage counselor, don't you see? Actually, I don't think he was a psychiatrist, which is a medical doctor, but a psychologist, a man with special training in psychology who isn't an M.D. But when that Mrs. Parsons began snooping into Sam's life, she got the story all wrong. That's what happens when you're predisposed to believe the worst about a man. You hear one little fact and blow it up out of all proportion. Mrs. Parsons learned that Sam had been paying visits to this psychologist and that was all she needed to know.

The way she twisted it in her mind, Sam was going through some sort of mental breakdown."

"Wow." Penny winced. "I never knew people could be so cruel."

"Well, I don't want to excuse her entirely, but I can see what made her act that way. She'd been scared to death by the accident and was doing what she thought she had to to prevent another one. Parents will go to extreme lengths to protect their kids, and Sam ended up being the scapegoat."

"But why didn't Sam simply tell the hearing about his divorce and the marriage counselor and all that?" Penny said, frowning with bafflement. "He could have cleared up the misunderstanding right then and there."

"It was harder for him than you think. To begin with, Sam's not one to talk about his private affairs. On top of that, he was in physical pain from the crash. At that moment he didn't feel capable of dredging up twenty-five years of misery. And even if he did, he didn't believe he could explain it satisfactorily to the hearing. He told me later he thought they would still have believed he was mentally unstable."

"Poor Sam," Penny said, biting her knuckles.

"As I said, between the accident and the divorce and all, Sam's lost his confidence. Unless and until he gets it back, I doubt if there's anything you can do for him—or he for you."

At that moment, despair descended on all three of them. They looked at one another through eyes clouded with futility. Heavily, David and Penny stood up, thanked Ken Sims, and trudged back to the bus stop.

12
Brainstorm

Lydia Carter's office in the court building in New Manchester was a cramped, glass-enclosed cubicle partitioned off from the large, dingy room reserved for defense lawyers and their clients. Her real office was located in another building down the street, but it was inconvenient to run over there every time she had to conduct an interview or review a brief, so she used the cubicle on days when she was in court. She had two different kinds of legal practice. She represented clients who could afford to pay a fee for her services, but she also acted as a court-appointed "defender" for people too poor to pay for legal help. The court did pay her a small sum for doing this, but that scarcely covered her expenses. She did it because she felt that underprivileged people deserved the same opportunity for a fair trial that well-to-do people had.

The receptionist had told Penny and David that Lydia would be returning from court any moment now and suggested they have a seat in her office. They made their way through a beehive of lawyers, clients, clerks, guards, witnesses, and a maze of desks and cubicles until they found the tiny enclosure with Lydia's name on it. There was hardly room to stand, let alone sit, but luckily Lydia came along a minute or two after they arrived.

Her eyebrows shot up. "Well, well, what a nice surprise." Then she squinted. "I hope you're not in any trouble. I've had my fill of thieves, vandals, and drunk-and-disorderlies today, thank you."

"I wish that were the kind of trouble we're in," David said, scuffing the floor with the toe of his shoe. "I'm certain you could help us there."

"Yes, this is a much tougher problem," Penny said.

"I see. Does it have to do with Sam?"

"Yes," they both answered together.

"I'll drive you home and you can tell me about it."

"Thanks, Lydia," said David. "It seems as if we've spent the whole day on one bus or another."

They went to the garage across the street from the state court building. Lydia got her old convertible and soon they were on the avenue leading out of New Manchester. "One good thing about being a lawyer is that the courts adjourn in midafternoon. I often get home before rush-hour traffic begins," she said. While waiting at a red light, she asked what was troubling them. They poured out everything they had learned since the last time they'd talked to her and told her about their conversation with Sam and his friend Ken. Lydia's legal mind could not tolerate imprecision, and she interrupted them a number of times to ask for clarification. "Now wait a minute," she'd say, "let me get this straight," or "Hold on, hold on, let's run over that again." The care with which she listened and asked questions made them feel she was genuinely interested in the case.

By the time they finished, the car had arrived in Aubrey Park and they were only a minute or two away from their home. "O.K.," Lydia said, "you've stated the problem. Now what's the solution?"

The kids looked at each other and then at her. "That's what we've come to *you* for!" said Penny.

"We've exhausted our ideas," David said. "We thought you might have some."

"For instance," said Penny, "couldn't you sue the school board to give Sam his job back?"

Lydia laughed. "Heavens, no! A lawyer can't sue someone by herself. She has to have a client."

"But Sam doesn't want to be a client," Penny objected.

"I realize that, but unless you can talk him into trying to get his job back, there's nothing I can do."

"Couldn't you go speak to him?" asked David.

"I'm afraid not. You see, lawyers have a code of ethical behavior, and one of the things they are not permitted to do is solicit clients—that is, ask to represent people. People have to come to them, not the other way around. Otherwise, you might have a lot of lawyers trying to drum up business like salesmen. It would destroy the principles on which our profession is based. But don't get me wrong. I think Sam's case is both interesting and important, and if he approached me I would be glad to represent him—even though I'm not sure he has enough evidence to win. On the other hand, as you said before, getting Sam's job back for him is only one issue; the other is publicizing your contention that Federal Motors is putting faulty brakes in its school buses. But getting Sam to come to me, or to any other attorney—well, I admit you've got a problem there, and I don't know how to solve it. If I think of anything, I'll let you know."

They'd been in front of the Case house for several minutes. The kids hung back from opening the door, as if an answer would come to them if they waited long enough. But none did and, with a depressed "Thanks, Lydia," they left the car.

Dinner was like a wake, and even the prospect of going with their parents to visit Vernon did not lighten the tone at the table. They related the day's events to their parents, half hoping Mr. and Mrs. Case would come up with an inspiration, but they only echoed Lydia's words: "I admit you've got a problem there."

Vernon was beaming when they walked into his room after dinner. "Good news. I spoke to the bus driver involved in that accident in Verona. He told me his brakes failed. He hit the pedal and there was a hiss and his foot went all the way to the floor. And it was a new Federal Motors bus."

Vernon was so pleased with himself that he didn't observe the lack of enthusiasm on the Case family's faces.

"He didn't know the lot number of the brakes and no one will tell him while the investigation is going on. Apparently, the school board is keeping everything hush-hush until they get to the bottom of the crash. So we still don't have proof positive, but at least we have a few more facts to add to our collection." The glow in his eyes faded as he realized his news was not being greeted with the excitement he'd expected. "Is there something the matter?"

The four Cases looked at one another, silently debating who was going to break the bad news to Vernon. Mr. Case was elected. "Vernon, I'm afraid we may have to drop our efforts."

He gaped. "Drop them! But . . . why?"

"We saw Sam today," David said. "He won't cooperate."

"Why not? Doesn't he want his job back?"

"He's afraid to try," said Penny, and briefly reviewed for Vernon their visits to Sam and Lydia.

Vernon scratched his head. "He must have been deeply hurt at that hearing."

"Don't remind me," Mr. Case said, looking unhappy.

"The thing is, Sam doesn't believe in himself anymore," Penny said.

"That's because he doesn't believe in *us,*" Mrs. Case pointed out. "He feels his friends in the community have let him down. What is worse, he feels they may let him down again. Right now, he is a social outcast. If you want to restore Sam's self-confidence, you'll have to restore his confidence in us."

"Well said," Mr. Case remarked, squeezing his wife's hand. "But the big question is, how?"

Mrs. Case thought for a moment and said, "I was reading in the paper today about a group of prisoners in a city jail who were social outcasts too. Then some reporter wrote an article —how did it describe them?—'forgotten men.' It said that nobody seemed to care about the squalid conditions and bad food, the brutality, the long time they spend behind bars waiting for their trials to begin. It stirred up community conscience. So a group of concerned people marched around the jail with picket signs protesting against abuses and reassuring the prisoners that they are not forgotten." Then Mrs. Case shrugged. "But I don't suppose you could do anything like that in Sam's case."

"Why not?" Penny asked, a faraway look in her eyes.

Mrs. Case laughed. "What are you going to do, picket for Sam?"

"Why not?" Penny repeated. "Everybody seems to be holding demonstrations these days. Why not us?"

A look of dismay came into her mother's eyes. "I don't like it. Too many things can go wrong. You'll get into trouble. There could be violence."

Penny looked at her. "You know what, Mother?"

"What?"

"You're talking just like a . . . a mother."

The same faraway look had come into David's and Vernon's eyes. "It's not the worst idea I've ever heard," David said. "It could kill two birds with one stone."

Vernon read his friend's mind. "Yes, it might convince Sam that we still care about him, and publicize the results of our investigation at the same time."

"I'm still not thrilled with it," Mrs. Case said.

The children looked at Mr. Case, who was nodding in tacit agreement with the plan. He winked at them as if to say, "Don't worry, I'll bring her around to our way of thinking."

Bringing Nurse Minster around proved far more difficult. The following afternoon during visiting hours she walked into Vernon's room and stopped dead in her tracks. "For the love of Mike, what's this?"

"This" was a squad of some fifteen children milling about

Vernon's bed. They all had pads and pencils and were scribbling notes, sipping sodas, or chewing candy bars while Vernon, Penny, and David barked out orders.

"Eddie, your job will be to check out the marching permit. You can work with Karen, who's drawing up the route. Got that, Karen?"

"Got it," a little red-haired girl said.

"Steve, you and Marjorie will be in charge of the picket signs and posters. Enlist as many kids as you need. Make 'em clever and artistic."

"What do we do for money?" Steve asked.

"Speak to David," Vernon said. "He's in charge of finances. We'll probably pass the hat, but we may be able to raise the balance from our parents."

"Do you want us to work on the other decorations too?" Steve wanted to know.

"No, you'll have your hands full with posters." He turned to Penny, who looked at the clipboard on her knees. "Yolanda and Mike are on decorations."

"Right. See David about money. Now, speaking of decorations, we have some dirty work and I'll have to ask for volunteers. We'll need a crew to clean up after the rally is over. We don't want to spoil the good we do by leaving litter all over the place. Do I hear any offers?"

Five hands went up. Penny took their names.

"Good," Vernon said. "And who would like to be our press secretary? We need someone to contact the newspapers, and maybe even magazines and television."

It was a choice assignment and eight hands went up. Vernon selected a girl named Carmen, who was editor of the school newspaper.

They discussed a number of other tasks and then strategy. Finally, Vernon said, "Can anyone think of something I've forgotten?"

The husky voice of Nurse Minster came from the door. "Yes, I can. You've forgotten that this is a hospital, young man."

The children shrank away from the imposing figure in white, who glowered at them with arms akimbo.

"It was the only way we could organize this thing," Vernon said meekly.

"I don't know what thing you're talking about, but I'd like to organize something myself. I'm asking for volunteers to stand up, walk through this door, take the elevator to the first floor, leave the building, and go home before a certain nurse, who is called The Monster behind her back, telephones the police."

She stepped aside as a stampede of children rushed for the door and spilled into the corridor.

Vernon, now alone, looked sheepishly at the nurse. "I'm sorry, Nurse Minster, but this meeting was critical."

"More critical than your injury, obviously. I think you're about ready to be released from this hospital."

"My only regret," Vernon said gallantly, "will be leaving you."

"Flattery will get you nowhere, buster." She went busily around the room, picking up cups and candy wrappers.

"Which reminds me," the patient said. "What makes you think anyone calls you The Monster behind your back?"

Nurse Minster stopped at his bedside, put her hands on her hips, and roared, "Because I *am* a monster!" sending Vernon scurrying under the sheets.

13

A Surprise Party

Many people believe that all suburbs are well-to-do, clean, beautiful places. Unfortunately, this belief can attract more people than the suburbs can support, and so a great many suburban towns have begun to experience the same problems that characterize our cities: poverty, inadequate housing, disease, and crime.

Aubrey Park was no exception. It had its Viaduct section, where large numbers of people had crowded into a small crescent of land that should have contained only one quarter their number. Men and women disappointed in their quest for a good job or cheap land or pleasant housing eventually ended up here.

One such individual was Sam Gilman.

Sam's personal situation had been declining ever since he and his wife had separated and divorced. Now that he lived by himself, he no longer needed a roomy apartment, nor was he inclined to do housework. So he had moved into a boarding house in the Viaduct. Then came the accident and loss of his job. He had not managed to save much money, because of the costliness of his divorce, so he was forced to collect unemployment insurance from the state. The weekly sum he received was so small that he had to find even cheaper and smaller quarters, a single room in a tenement where cockroaches and even rats were commonly seen. His only pleasure in life now was his visits to the Veterans of Foreign Wars Lodge, but lately even these were becoming a source of shame to him. He could not keep up appearances and everybody there knew what poor circumstances he was living in. He was too proud to suffer the pitying looks of the other members.

He had spent the morning looking for a job, but as usual with no success. All prospective employers asked him what he had been doing before and requested references or recommendations. Naturally, he could not refer them to the school board which had fired him for negligence. So Sam found himself trapped in a vicious circle. He could not get a job without a reference, but if he referred prospective employers to the school board, he would never get a job. Sam ate a meager lunch and surveyed the future. It was dreadfully bleak. Unemployment insurance did not last forever. When the benefits to which he was entitled ran out, he would go on welfare, making him the recipient of a form of charity. To a man who had once owned a fleet of trucks, this prospect was unbearable.

Luckily, this train of thought was interrupted by a knock

on the door of his shabby room. "Who's there?" he asked life-lessly.

"It's me, Sam. Ken."

Sam shuffled to the door and undid the two locks and a chain that guarded his quarters against intruders. Although he had nothing worth stealing, he had heard of desperate men breaking into rooms like his own just to steal a few threadbare clothes, an old watch, a pair of shoes.

Ken Sims beamed and entered. Through every step of Sam's ordeal Ken had remained loyal, lending his good-na-tured support when things appeared darkest for his com-panion. Ken had also lent Sam money, though Sam had ar-gued strenuously that he could not envision the day when he'd be able to pay it back. Why, if it had not been for Ken . . . Sam shuddered to think what would have become of him by this time.

"Well now, Sam, how's it going today?" Ken asked. One of the things Ken did was to make believe nothing was wrong.

To preserve his own pride, Sam played along with these lit-tle deceptions. "Oh, well enough. I spoke to the personnel manager of that bakery today. He says that delivery-truck job looks pretty good. He's just got to check with the head of the company."

"That's great. You'll be back in shape in no time. How about a card game down at the lodge?"

Sam sat with hunched shoulders on the edge of his bed. "I don't think so today, Ken. I . . . I have to stick around here in case the bakery people try to get in touch with me about that job."

"Oh, they can leave a message for you if they want you badly enough."

"I guess. But I'm a bit tired anyway. Maybe tomorrow."

"If it's a matter of money, we're playing for very low stakes and I can advance you what you need."

Sam shook his head. He didn't want to be deeper in debt to Ken, who after all needed money himself. Besides, Sam was beginning to suspect his friends of letting him win at cards so that they could bestow money on him without damaging his pride.

Normally, Ken would have dropped the subject, but today he was curiously persistent. "Aw, come on, Sam, they're all asking for you. They say it's just not the same game without you."

"Now, Ken, stop trying to cheer me up with all these fibs. Everybody knows I'm washed up. I'm no fun at all, just sitting around feeling sorry for myself. In fact, I don't know why *you* bother with me anymore."

Ken got indignant. "Why, Sam Gilman, you mustn't think very much of me if you believe I'd turn my back on you just because you ran into a spot of trouble."

"A spot? Listen, I'm at the end of the line. The next step for me is to become a panhandler, begging for dimes on the streets."

Now Ken was fighting mad. He grabbed Sam by his shirt and pulled him to his feet. "The next step for you, mister, is to come down to the lodge with me this very second. I may be fifty pounds overweight, but I can still beat the stuffing out of you, so don't test my patience any further."

Sam scratched the back of his skull. "I don't know why you're going to so much trouble for me, but all right."

"Good. Now shave, comb your hair, and put on a fresh shirt."

Sam stared at him. "What for? They've seen me this way before." He ran his hand over his food-stained shirt, the three-day stubble on his cheeks, and the dry tangle of hair on his head.

"Well, you see, there's this . . . uh . . . party, sort of. Everyone is sprucing up a little extra."

Sam shrugged, but shaved, put a little oil on his hair and brushed it neatly, and changed into a clean shirt.

"You wouldn't want to put a tie and jacket on too, would you?" Ken asked, knowing what the answer would be.

"Heck no. For a measly little card game?"

"Yeah. Well, maybe I'll carry them for you just in case."

"In case what? What's going on down there, a visit from the President of the United States?"

"You'll see." Ken took a tie and jacket out of Sam's closet and pushed his friend out the door before Sam had a chance to change his mind.

They walked down the street and under the raised highway that gave the Viaduct section its name. The VFW Lodge was several blocks away. As they approached, Ken Sims kept looking at his watch. By this time, Sam had the feeling that something extraordinary was going on, but he couldn't imagine what. As they rounded a corner he saw a crowd of people carrying colorful pennants, banners, and signs, milling around outside the lodge. "Say, Ken, what's going on?"

"As I said, you'll see. Are you sure you don't want to put this tie and jacket on?" He had a smirk on his face.

"Why on earth would I want to do that? Hmmm, what does that sign say?" He squinted. " 'Parents, Are You Sending Us to School in Death Traps?' " Sam read. He saw another picket sign. " 'School Board, Get Your Head Out of the Sand.' " He turned to Ken. "What's this all about?"

Ken pointed to a third sign. "Read that one. It'll tell you."

" 'Give Sam His Job Back,' " Sam read. "Sam . . . you mean —me?"

Just as Ken was about to answer, someone in the crowd spotted him coming. "Here he is! It's Sam! Sam's coming!"

Suddenly a band struck up and the crowd began to cheer, and now the full extent of the demonstration made itself clear. At least a hundred schoolchildren milled in the street, and scores of lodge members in their uniforms stood on the porch outside the hall. Many of the people carried signs or bedsheets with slogans demanding that the school board give Sam his job back, that there be an investigation of the brakes of all school buses in the Aubrey Park district, and that Federal Motors examine its products for potentially fatal defects. Draped over the door of the lodge was a huge banner proclaiming, "WE LOVE YOU, SAM," and beneath it an eight-man band, combining schoolchildren and puffing lodge members, played a bouncy march.

"Ken, I see it, but I still don't understand it," Sam gasped.

"You just make your way up to the front of the lodge and you'll understand soon enough." The crowd parted in front of Sam, giving him an avenue straight through to the front steps of the hall.

"O.K., but give me my tie and jacket. I can't go up there looking like this!"

He donned his tie and jacket and strode through the cheering assembly. A number of press photographers stepped into his path and took pictures, and he observed a television camera crew from New Manchester on top of a station wagon recording the event on videotape.

His mind told him what was going on, but he still couldn't explain it, and he wasn't sure he'd believe it even if he could. People he had never seen before were shaking his hand or patting him on the back, saying, "We're with you, Sam."

He reached the steps. At the top, a number of lodge officers stood with David and Penny Case, Vernon Stevenson in a gaily decorated wheelchair, and two other students holding what looked like a heavy roll of paper. A microphone had been set up with loudspeakers pointing left, right, and straight ahead.

Everyone applauded as Sam, with as much dignity as he could muster on such short notice, trotted up the steps. When he reached the top he waved his hands, eliciting a cheer that lasted several minutes. Still dazed and confused, he stood uncertainly, allowing the others to take charge. Major Fitzroy, one of the lodge officers, beckoned to Sam and led him to the microphone. There Sam shook a lot of hands while Major Fitzroy waved his arms to silence the throng.

When the cheering finally died down, the Major leaned into the microphone and said, "Thank you, thank you all for coming down here to honor Sam Gilman. Sam has been a member in good standing of our lodge for some twenty-five years. During that time he has served our community well. Recently, however, he was involved in an accident and dismissed from his job after an investigation by the Aubrey Park school board. The board determined that Sam had been negligent, but a diligent group of students has been investigating the charge and the accident and has come up with a very different interpretation. It is not for us to say whether that interpretation is the correct one or not. But I speak officially for the officers and membership of this lodge when I say that it has enough merit to warrant a reopening of Sam's case. Not only do we believe Sam may have lost his job for no good reason; we also believe that a greater tragedy may be shaping up. Because if the claims made by these students are valid, then our schoolchildren are riding around in unsafe buses. And so we urge the school board to reconsider its hasty action and to examine carefully the information these kids have brought to light."

Another cheer went up. Sam felt a constriction in his throat and looked embarrassedly around him. His eyes focused on Penny Case, who stepped up to the microphone and asked the crowd to calm down. Behind her, the two students bearing the thick roll of paper drew more and more attention as Penny addressed Sam, glancing at a note in her hand from time to time.

"Sam, the students, as well as many parents, of the Aubrey Park school district would like you to know that they deplore the severe action taken by the school board in dismissing you from your job. In the weeks that have passed since that action, a number of important facts have come to light. We believe that it is imperative that the board examine these facts. We have therefore circulated a petition among the children and adults of Aubrey Park to this effect. We have got 2,143 signatures on it and are happy to present it to you now." To the roar of the crowd, the two students stepped forward and placed the heavy roll of paper in Sam's hands.

"Speech!" someone yelled. "We want Sam!" a little knot of children began chanting. It was quickly picked up by more and more people. "We want Sam! We want Sam!" Soon the entire crowd was roaring in a single voice, "We want Sam! We want Sam! We want Sam!"

"Sam, please say something to them," Penny begged him.

Someone nudged Sam forward, but he planted his heels like a stubborn mule. The chanting grew louder and more insistent. In spite of his reluctance, he realized he had to say something to the people who had gone to so much trouble to show their faith in him. He stepped forward, clutching the microphone as if it were a dangerous snake. The crowd grew silent expectantly.

His face was flushed dark red with embarrassment, and for a moment after he opened his mouth nothing came out. Then, clearing his throat, he said, "I . . . I want to apologize to you."

"No, no!" a number of people shouted. "You don't owe us any apologies, Sam."

"Yes I do. I've been thinking selfishly of myself instead of the children. I've been feeling pity for myself instead of feeling it for the kids who might one day end up crippled or worse because I didn't speak out. I don't deserve what you've done for me today."

"Yes you do, Sam," several called.

"No, if anyone deserves credit, it's these kids who have stuck their necks out in the last couple of weeks to get at the truth."

Sam gestured in the direction of David, Penny, and Vernon, and a loud cheer went up. The three youngsters looked down modestly.

"These children have asked me to try to get my job back. And from the looks of this petition, a lot of other people want me to try too. Well, I want to tell you I'm going to do

just that. Now hold on," he quickly said as the audience broke into applause. "Hold on. I want to make it clear that I'm not doing this for myself. To tell you the truth, I'm not sure at this point whether I want the job, or even if I'm qualified to drive a bus anymore. The reason I'm doing this is to . . . uh . . . publicize what I've been saying all along, namely that the brakes on my bus failed. They may fail again. They may fail on some of the other buses being used in this school district. They may fail on some of the buses being driven in other school districts. I feel I owe it to you to try to force the powers that be to check out my claim. So I just want to say thank you, friends. I'm going to keep the faith this time."

A deafening roar went up that lasted for several minutes. Then David stepped up to the microphone and said, "O.K., everybody, we're going to proceed to the elementary school to present our petition officially to the school board. Let's make it orderly and peaceful. Ready? Follow us."

Vernon's wheelchair glided down a plank ramp. David and Penny, flanking Sam, followed him. Behind them the two students bearing the petition scroll took their places, followed by the marching band, the uniformed lodge members, and the rest of the crowd.

Vernon, who had been released from the hospital the previous day, to the relief of a certain stout nurse, had managed to commandeer his souped-up wheelchair for the occasion. He had hastily modified it to remove the technical "bugs," and as the long line assembled behind him, he flipped a switch on one of the arms and the chair lurched forward, its speed and direction carefully controlled by a rudder-like device he had installed. The band struck up a brisk march, and the crowd surged down the street, cheering, laughing, and chanting. There was only one unpleasant incident: sour-faced Mrs. Parsons barged into the street to drag her son Raymond out of the parade.

The march wound its way through the streets of Aubrey Park along a route approved by the town council. The marchers waved their placards and signs at passersby and invited them to join the parade. A number did, and the ranks had swollen substantially by the time they entered the school grounds. As it was a Saturday, there were no classes, but a number of children were playing on the baseball diamond and track, and they all rushed to the entrance to see what was going on. At this point Vernon announced to Sam, David, and Penny that it was time for his *pièce de résistance.*

Before they could determine what he meant, Vernon had flipped several switches on his wheelchair. Suddenly the chair seemed to go mad. Two American flags on the back started waving back and forth, a sign between them that said "WE LOVE YOU, SAM" moved up and down, pinwheels on the sides started spinning gay colors, and several strings of ladyfinger firecrackers started popping. The crowd went wild and for five minutes stood before the school doors calling for the school board to come out and accept the petition.

Sam leaned over the wheelchair with a troubled look. "With all your genius for organization, I'm afraid you've forgotten the most important thing of all, son."

"What's that?"

"There's no member of the school board present to accept your petition."

Vernon looked over his shoulder and winked at Penny and David. "Well, Sam, maybe a miracle will happen."

They turned their attention back to the school doors. Suddenly a figure appeared within, opened the doors, and stepped out.

"Why, it's Mr. Case!" Sam cried.

"Fancy that," Vernon said with a grin.

Again the crowd roared for several minutes. Mr. Case raised his hands, signaling for silence. The noise at last subsided and Mr. Case addressed the crowd. "I understand you want to present a petition to the school board."

"Yes, yes, yes," they chanted.

"By the strangest of coincidences, I just happened to be in the school this afternoon. And I am a member of the school board."

They cheered.

"Therefore, on behalf of the board, I will be happy to accept your petition and present it to my colleagues."

He beckoned to David, Penny, Sam, and the two students bearing the petition. They stepped up to the school doors and placed the scroll in Mr. Case's hands.

Although the cheering almost drowned out his voice, Sam put his mouth close to Mr. Case's ear and said, "Mighty peculiar, you being here just when we needed a member of the school board."

"Isn't it?" Mr. Case replied. "Why, if you didn't know better, you might think it was planned this way." And he vanished through the doors as mysteriously as he had appeared.

14
Lydia Takes Charge

That evening Sam, accompanied by Penny and David, paid a visit to the home of Ralph and Lydia Carter. Vernon had wanted to accompany them, but the day's activities had exhausted him and, with the aid of Vernon's parents, they had ganged up on him and made him stay in bed.

The evening was warm and sultry, hinting that summer was fast approaching. Lydia's famous lemonade was a welcome refreshment.

"Just like Penny and David said, this has to be the best lemonade I've ever tasted," Sam said, offering his glass for a refill.

"It's the mint," Lydia replied. "I grow it in the backyard."

"The kids also said you're the greatest lawyer they've ever met."

"I believe I'm the *only* lawyer they've ever met," Lydia said with a laugh.

Sam washed the lemonade around his glass as if searching for a tactful way to phrase his next question. "Tell me, do you experience any, uh, trouble? I mean, being a woman and . . . uh . . ."

"Black? Everyone asks me that question, Sam. Especially prospective clients."

"Oh, don't get me wrong," he said, flustered.

"What you want to know is whether a black female lawyer will be as effective as a white male."

"No, no," Sam protested. But he waited for her answer.

"I've run up against prejudice from time to time, I won't deny it. Some people don't think black people should be lawyers. Others don't think women should be lawyers. And still others think one or the other is O.K., but that the combination is fatal. On the other hand, there are just as many, maybe even more, who think it's a fine thing. And some in my profession have gone out of their way to make sure they treated me fairly. They balance the prejudiced ones. The point is, Sam, that neither my sex nor my color has hampered me in the practice of law. My won-and-lost record, as they say in baseball, is considerably over .500."

"I'm afraid I've given you the wrong impression," Sam protested.

"No, you've given the impression of a person who is calculating his chances of winning his case. All in all, that's a healthy sign, considering how discouraged you were a week ago."

"Well, then let's get on with this question of winning," Sam said. "But let me just warn you right off the bat that I don't have a penny to pay you with. If we win this lawsuit, of course, and I'm rehired, there'll be my salary, such as it is, but . . ."

"Suppose we skip the question of my fee for the moment. Bear in mind that I undertake a great many legal services without charge. And when the issue is not just your job but the safety of large numbers of children, I can assure you that a fee is of secondary importance to me."

Sam listened intently.

"One word which is commonly overused by people who go to lawyers is 'sue,'" Lydia explained. "There is far more to law than lawsuits, Sam, and there are a number of approaches to this case that don't require going to court."

Penny and David looked baffled and slightly disappointed. "How else can we win our fight if we don't sue?" Penny asked.

"There are countless ways of adjudicating grievances, to use the legal phrase. Believe it or not, the lawsuit is not the most common. Lawsuits are expensive, time-consuming, risky, involved, and frustrating affairs. Although the legal profession earns much of its living from them, most lawyers will tell their clients to do all they can to avoid a suit, even if the clients are positive they can win. Some jurists have likened lawsuits to war: only when all other peaceful means have failed should one litigate, or go to court."

"I'm still not sure I understand," Penny said. "What other ways do we have to—what was it you said?—adjudicate our grievance?"

"Well," said Lydia, "sometimes the mere threat of a suit

will achieve the desired action. By warning someone that you are considering legal action, you can get him to meet his obligations. He may not want to incur the cost of hiring a lawyer, or spend a lot of time in court, or risk a very expensive loss in court when he can meet his responsibilities less expensively at the outset. Still other people don't want to be exposed to the publicity of a lawsuit."

"That would be especially true of Federal Motors, wouldn't it?" David said.

"Yes, it might be. Another thing to bear in mind is that even if you should have to resort to a lawsuit, your differences can be settled out of court before an official decision has been rendered."

"I've heard that phrase 'settled out of court,' but I never quite knew what it meant," said Penny.

"It simply means that the people involved in the dispute decide to resolve their differences by negotiating with each other, instead of waiting for a third party—a judge, or jury, or some other adjudicating body—to settle it for them."

"A compromise?" Penny asked.

"Yes, that's it exactly. A compromise."

"Why would they compromise after going to court?" David wanted to know.

"Maybe the case is costing them too much money. Maybe they fear they're going to lose. Maybe the bad publicity is damaging their public image. Maybe they're simply weary. Remember that our legal system entitles those who lose a case to appeal to a higher court, and if they lose in that higher court, there are several still higher, right up to the Supreme Court. But pursuing your case up that chain of appeals can take years and a fortune. So, when you think about it, relatively few legal disputes go the full distance."

"I hope ours won't drag on," Sam said.

"If we handle it right," Lydia reassured him, "there's no reason why it should go to court at all."

"How *are* you going to handle it, dear?" Ralph asked with genuine curiosity. Despite years of married life, he frequently found himself completely in the dark as to what was in his wife's mind.

"Well," said Lydia, who obviously had been giving the matter a great deal of thought, "if by threatening to sue we can force the school board to reopen its investigation of the brakes, we'll be halfway there. Perhaps we don't even have to threaten to sue. That petition you presented them with today might do the trick."

"Yes, but most of the names on it are those of schoolchildren," David pointed out. "I don't imagine they'll carry much weight among the members of the school board."

"I disagree. Student power being what it is these days, I believe the board will take the petition seriously, especially because it is a responsible document representing serious investigation. I'm certain that many parents will be gravely concerned as a result of it, and when *they* begin putting pressure on the board, you will see results."

"Wow, I didn't think we'd accomplished that much," Penny said with a whistle.

"I don't think you realize how much you've accomplished. Your demonstration was well covered by the press, meaning it will be brought to the attention of Federal Motors and the State Motor Vehicle Bureau. If we succeed in getting the school board to reopen hearings, we will be able to bring Federal Motors and state officials into the act. When that happens, I believe you'll see the machinery of justice begin to turn under its own power, instead of requiring the push we're giving it." Lydia sat back, sipped her lemonade, and let all this information sink into the minds of her company.

Sam had retreated into meditation and seemed almost detached from the proceedings. But now attention focused on him, and Penny asked the question that was in everybody else's mind.

"Well, Sam? What do you think?"

He turned to Penny and David. "I think you may be right."

"Right?" the girl asked. "About what?"

"About Mrs. Carter here being the best lawyer I've ever met. And believe me," he said, smiling at Lydia, "you're not the only one I've ever met. So—when do we begin?"

"As soon as I've spoken to the school board on Monday," said Lydia. "Meanwhile, we have some homework to do. There are a number of factual gaps in our case which must be filled before I will feel confident we can win. I'll make some notes tomorrow and give you your assignments tomorrow evening. Meanwhile, Sam, I want you to let me know if anyone tries to contact you, besides one of us, I mean."

Sam frowned. "Anyone? I'm not sure I know who you mean."

"I'm not sure myself," Lydia replied cryptically. "But I have a feeling you're going to be a popular man in the next couple of weeks."

15
Unexpected Visitors

Lydia's intuition proved amazingly accurate. The very next evening as Sam was finishing the article about the demonstration in the *New Manchester Sunday Telegram,* there was a knock on his door. He asked who was there but could not make out the reply. The voice did not sound unfriendly and he opened the door the width of the chain lock.

There were two smiling, well-dressed men standing in the hallway. "Mr. Gilman?" the taller one asked.

"Yes?"

"May we come in? I'm Mr. Austin and this is Mr. Marley. We're from Federal Motors."

Sam felt the hair on the back of his neck prickling. Lydia Carter's warning echoed through his mind. He did not wish to seem rude, yet he was reluctant to invite them in. His good manners finally prevailed, and he undid the chain lock, saying, "If you can stand it, you're welcome."

They carefully ignored the cracked plaster, dismal lighting, and cheap, rickety furniture, but when Sam offered them tea or coffee, they declined.

"We'll get to the point at once, Mr. Gilman," said Mr. Austin. "We've been following the—uh—matter of your accident in the newspapers. That was quite a display your friends put on for you yesterday. I saw it on last night's TV news. Obviously they're very fond of you."

"I guess," Sam said cautiously, wondering what they were leading up to.

"As we understand the demonstration, its purpose was to reopen hearings on your handling of that bus."

"That's right. I've denied my negligence all along. I'm claiming that something went wrong with the brakes of my bus."

"That's a very serious charge, Mr. Gilman. You're aware of course that the bus was a Federal Motors product."

"I am, Mr. Austin."

"The papers say you are claiming that Federal Motors manufactured a faulty vehicle," Mr. Marley said.

"Read the papers again," Sam said, tapping the article on the table in front of him. "I only said I have reason to believe it *may* have been faulty."

"Perhaps you don't realize it, Mr. Gilman, but there are laws against making irresponsible claims like that in public. You can be sued for damaging our public image."

"Only if my claims do turn out to be irresponsible," Sam

answered irritably. He now began to catch the drift of their visit. They were trying to intimidate him.

"The burden of proof rests with you," Mr. Austin said. Then he leaned back, affecting relaxation, and smiled confidently. "You know, Sam—if I may call you Sam—we've been in the automotive business a long, long time. Federal Motors is dedicated to safety and reliability. And that is doubly true when it comes to vehicles designed to carry children. To say that we would permit school buses to be built and put on the road knowing that they are defective . . ."

"Wait a minute. I haven't said you knew about any defects. Quite the opposite. I'm saying there may be a defect you don't know about."

"That's out of the question," Mr. Austin answered sternly. "Why, a respected engineer—Mr. Case—tested the bus after the accident and the results were negative. And our own engineers have run a few tests too. There is nothing wrong with our brakes."

"Then you have nothing to worry about, do you?" said Sam, smiling. Now that he knew what their mission was, he was beginning to feel more confident. "Which leads me to ask what brings you here. After all, if I'm making irresponsible claims, all you have to do is prove me wrong or sue me for damaging your company's reputation."

The two public relations men looked at each other with a touch of anxiety. Then Mr. Austin said, "Of course, if you know something that we do not . . ."

"That will be brought out if and when the hearings are reopened," Sam said firmly. "And if you want any further information on that score, you'll have to contact my attorney."

The two visitors stiffened. "Ah, you've engaged an attorney, then?" said Mr. Austin.

"That's right," Sam said, feeling growing command of the interview.

There was a pause as Austin and Marley exchanged looks. They seemed to be trying by means of mental telepathy to formulate their next tactic. At length Mr. Austin smiled unctuously. Sam felt the muscles in his stomach tighten up. There was something about the man's smile that made him terribly uncomfortable. "Now look, Sam, all this talk of lawyers and suits seems completely unnecessary. What is it you want, really? You want your job back, right? And I imagine you want the salary you lost since you were dismissed."

Sam decided not to say anything, but to let Austin speak.

"If that's all that's involved, it's the easiest thing in the world to straighten out. We have a lot of influence in this town. I'm sure that a few well-chosen words to the right people in the right places would smooth the way with a minimum of fuss and publicity. What do you say to that?"

Sam stood up abruptly. "I say it's way past my bedtime, gentlemen."

"Now see here, Sam . . ."

"It's 'Mr. Gilman' to you, Mr. Austin."

"Don't be unreasonable," Marley said, getting reluctantly to his feet and moving toward the door.

"I'm afraid you don't appreciate what's at stake," Sam said, holding the door for them. "This thing is bigger than my job. Much bigger."

"Then what is it?" Mr. Austin asked.

"I'm doing this for the schoolchildren," Sam said proudly. "As you can see, I don't have anything left to lose, at least not anything material. But I do have a few principles, and a man's not a man if he gives those up without a fight."

Mr. Austin shook his head. "I'm afraid I don't understand. But if it's a fight you're looking for, we'll give you one."

"You know what, Mr. Austin? I'm looking forward to it." And he shut the door in their faces with deep satisfaction.

16

The Hearing

Ralph Carter looked forlornly at the plateful of bacon and eggs that sat uneaten in front of his wife. "I should have known better than to make you breakfast this morning."

"I'm sorry," Lydia said, looking up from her brief. "I've been so involved in this case I forgot to tell you to skip my breakfast. I tried a little bit of the bacon, but . . . well, you know I'm just too nervous to eat on days like this."

Ralph reached for her plate and consumed its contents. "Funny, but my reaction is just the opposite. When I get nervous I eat like a starving man."

"The way you're eating now?" Lydia laughed.

"I'm nervous now—for your sake. Besides, I love bacon and eggs." He sipped some coffee and said, "Actually, I don't see what there is to be anxious about. After all, this isn't a trial. It's just a hearing."

"Yes, but there's an awful lot riding on the outcome. On top of which, I'm far from confident. Our evidence is too thin. If I were presiding over this hearing, I'd throw my own case out. That's what's really got me uptight."

"I'm sure you're exaggerating," her husband assured her. "You say that before every showdown."

"I've never meant it more. And where are those children? They were supposed to be here at eight thirty."

"It's only eight twenty-five. Keep cool, darling."

Moments later the doorbell rang and it was David, Penny, and Vernon. They were dressed presentably for their appearance before the State Highway Safety Board hearing. But Lydia frowned when she inspected Vernon, who was on crutches.

"What's the matter?" he asked anxiously, following Lydia's eyes down his trouser legs to his foot. "You mean my cast? There's nothing I can do about that. I have to wear one for at least another . . ."

"Oh, I understand that, but do you have to display all those gaudy signatures?" Indeed, the cast had been signed in rainbow colors, with many highly artistic touches. "It's very nice for display in a museum of modern art, but I'm not sure how it will go in a solemn hearing. I wouldn't want anyone to think you're a capricious person."

"Yes, I hadn't thought of that." He shut his eyes for a second. "Let's see, it's too big for a sock . . ." Then he snapped his fingers. "Ralph, that dark blue knit stocking cap you wear to school in the winter—do you still have it?"

"Sure. It's in the front closet. I'll get it."

"I think we'll need a large rubber band, too."

Thus with Ralph Carter's stocking cap secured with a rubber band over his cast, Vernon hobbled out to Lydia's car, followed by Lydia, David, and Penny.

Lydia eased the car into the heavy rush-hour traffic that drifted like a sluggish river into the city. "Well, kids, how do you feel?" Lydia asked, trying to conceal her own nervousness.

"Eager," said Vernon.

"Scared," said David.

"Confused," said Penny.

"I can understand the first two, but not the third. What's confusing you, Penny?"

"I'm not sure I understand who's holding the hearing and what it's all about. I mean, is it like a trial or what?"

"She told you it's not a trial," David said, nudging his sister impatiently with his elbow.

She nudged him back with considerably more force. "Look, it's no great crime if I'm confused about something, is it?"

"She's right, David," Lydia interceded. "This isn't a cut-and-dried formal legal action. It's an administrative proceeding and therefore a bit more casual and discretionary. That is, the rules aren't clearly defined by law. So I can't blame Penny for being uncertain about what to expect."

Vindicated, Penny stuck her tongue out at her brother.

"Let's just review the situation briefly. Last week, after your demonstration, I spoke to Mr. Twilly, chairman of the school board, on the phone. I told him that since Sam's dismissal we had collected new evidence to support Sam's contention that the brakes failed. Of course, Mr. Twilly was aware of this because of the petition you had presented to the board. I asked Mr. Twilly, therefore, to conduct another hearing to reconsider Sam's dismissal. I warned him—politely, of course—that if the board refused, I would initiate a lawsuit to compel that hearing."

"And what did he say?" Penny asked.

"He said there was no need for that. The school board, with one exception, was very impressed with your petition and was as eager to get to the truth of the matter as we are."

"I'll bet the exception was crabby Mrs. Parsons," Penny said.

"I'm afraid so," Lydia confirmed. "But Mr. Twilly had an excellent suggestion. He said that since this is not just a question of one bus, but possibly a great many, we ought to take it up with the State Highway Safety Board. If that agency finds merit in Sam's claim, Mr. Twilly will be delighted to hold a new hearing on Sam's dismissal."

"So you contacted the State Highway Safety Board?" said David.

"Yes. Interestingly, they had been looking into the matter themselves as a result of the publicity your demonstration got."

"Hey, that's great," David beamed.

"I knew that would please you," said Lydia. "Anyway, the State Highway Safety Board is an informal, information-gathering group that makes recommendations to the State Motor Vehicle Bureau. It's the bureau that has decisive power in these matters, so it's important that we make the strongest possible impression today. Because now the emphasis is not just on Sam's job, but on the safety of a whole fleet of buses being used around the country. And that's what we've been trying to establish. Even Sam himself doesn't care that much whether or not he gets his job back, as long as the issue of brake safety is thoroughly aired before a responsible public body. Still confused?" Lydia asked Penny.

"No," she answered. "Now I'm eager like Vernon—and scared like David."

"There's good reason for being both," the lawyer said.

"Which are you?"

"Frankly, I'm worried. There's too much straw in our case and not enough bricks."

The children frowned.

The State Motor Vehicle Bureau was a fairly new building in the heart of the civic center of New Manchester. The hearing was scheduled for 9:30 in a large conference room on the second floor. They arrived in the lobby at 9:15 and looked for Sam under the large clock, where they'd agreed to meet. He was there, looking better than he'd looked in months, in a neatly pressed suit, shoes shined, hair combed, and face freshly shaven. His eyes had the pleasant twinkle that had characterized them in the old days before his troubles began. His arm was still in a sling; his cast had been removed earlier in the week, but Lydia had instructed him to use the sling anyway. "It will attract sympathy for you," she'd said with a wise smile.

They greeted one another, then Lydia looked around. "Where's Mr. Cassiday? If he doesn't show up, we're just about lost."

David looked around the lobby. "Isn't that he over there, standing behind that newspaper?"

"What's he hiding for?" Penny said, looking incredu-

lously at the Federal Motors engineer, who was peering furtively over the paper.

"Maybe he doesn't want to be seen by the other gents from Federal Motors," Sam suggested. "At least not until the hearing begins."

"I'm still not sure I get it," said Penny.

"You will," Lydia answered, leading them over to Mr. Cassiday. He jumped when she addressed him.

"Oh, it's you," he said with visible relief.

"I'm so glad you could come," Lydia said. "I can't tell you how terribly important it is that you testify for us this morning."

"To tell you the truth, I almost didn't come. This morning I got an acute case of cold feet."

"That's one of the things that's been worrying me," Lydia said, looking brighter. "After all, you're risking your job by appearing on our behalf."

"Yes," he said with a grim smile. "And that will make me an unemployed hero. I'm not sure I wouldn't rather be an employed coward."

"Like your associates who are going to be here this morning, Austin and Marley?" Sam asked, with a trace of cynicism.

"You sound like you know them," the long-haired engineer laughed.

"I do. They paid me a visit last week."

David, Penny, and Vernon looked astonished. "They did?" all three exclaimed at once.

"Yes. I told Mrs. Carter here about it."

"You didn't tell us," Penny said with a mild look of betrayal.

"I'm sorry, I've been too busy," Lydia explained. She then

related what Sam had told her about the visit by the two Federal Motors public relations men.

"You don't think they're covering something up, do you?" David asked.

"No, I don't," Lydia answered. "I'm certain they believe our claims are not valid. But being public relations men, they realize that whether our claims are valid or not, their company's image is going to be hurt by the publicity. People tend to believe bad things about large corporations quicker than good things, and to remember them longer. By visiting Sam, Austin and Marley were only doing their job, trying to prevent harmful publicity before it starts. Well," she said, looking at the big clock, "I guess we should get going."

They took an elevator to the second floor and found room 216. The door was open and they paused to survey the room before entering. The children, who could not get it out of their heads that this was a trial, expected something resembling a courtroom. Actually it was nothing like one; it was only a large rectangular room with a long table surrounded by some twenty chairs. All in all it looked like a room in which very businesslike meetings were conducted.

Some of the people in the room were familiar to Penny, David, and Vernon. On one side of the table were Mr. Case, smiling warmly at them; Mrs. Parsons, frowning; several members of the school board; and Mr. Twilly, the board's chairman.

Opposite the school-board members were Mr. Austin and Mr. Marley, the two public relations men who had shown them around the Federal Motors building, along with two very conservatively dressed young men, whom the children figured to be lawyers. Mr. Austin and Mr. Marley had their cordial smiles on display, as usual, but their lawyers looked very earnest.

At the head of the table facing them was a sharp-faced man in his mid-forties, flanked by a pipe-smoking gentleman and a young, pretty woman. Behind them sat an older woman, whose hands rested on a stenographic machine.

The man at the head of the table rose and gestured to Lydia and the others to take seats at the opposite end of the table, near the door. At the sight of Cassiday, the mouths of Austin and Marley dropped open. After a moment Mr. Austin said, "I wasn't aware you'd been invited to testify, but why don't you sit over here with us?"

The young engineer blushed with embarrassment. He shrugged his shoulders and said in an almost inaudible voice, "Uh, thanks, but I'll be sitting over here with Mrs. Carter."

The public relations men leaned over and consulted in whispers with their attorneys but said nothing further about Cassiday's extraordinary appearance.

At a gesture from the man at the head of the table, Mr. Case closed the door. At once everyone in the room quieted down. The man at the head of the table scanned the faces quickly, like someone thumbing through a book to get an instant idea of who the characters are and what the story is about. Then he said, "My name is Peter Eggleston and I'm head of the Highway Safety Board of the State Motor Vehicle Bureau. This gentleman at my left is Dr. Cordell, one of our consulting engineers, and the lady at my right is Mrs. Dorn, assistant to the head of our investigative division. Behind me is Mrs. Laski, who will be recording the testimony given here today."

Mr. Eggleston briefly read the names of the others at the table, then said, "Although you are all familiar with the facts of this case, it might be a good idea for me to summarize them at this time, both to refresh our memories and to enter them on the official records of this hearing.

"On Tuesday, April 17th of this year, after dropping off all but one of his passengers at the end of the school day, driver Sam Gilman lost control of his bus as it was approaching Mason Street from the west, on the Temple Avenue hill that leads into Aubrey Park. The bus went through a red light, rammed a gardener's truck moving in the same direction, jumped the curb, and hit the side of the Better Brands Supermarket. Mr. Gilman and his passenger, Vernon Stevenson"—he nodded at Sam and Vernon—"were injured, and the bus, truck, and supermarket property were damaged.

"A hearing was held by the Aubrey Park school board, Mr. Twilly presiding. It heard two conflicting claims. One, by the driver Sam Gilman, was that the bus brakes had failed to respond on the Temple Avenue hill. The second was that Mr. Gilman had been driving recklessly, and was even possibly drunk."

Sam Gilman flinched but held his emotions in check.

"The suggestion of drunkenness was dismissed as groundless. However, because tests on the bus brakes after the accident produced no indication of failure, the school board concluded that Mr. Gilman, though not drunk, was nevertheless reckless for some other reason. It was brought out at the time that Mr. Gilman had been emotionally troubled for some months before the accident, and at the time of the accident was under the care of a psychiatrist. The school board determined that there was no justifiable excuse for his losing control of the bus and dismissed him from employment." Mr. Eggleston looked around. "Does anyone wish to correct my description of the events?"

No one indicated an objection, and Mr. Eggleston continued. "Subsequent to his dismissal, a team of young students, including the one injured in the accident, Vernon Stevenson, decided to investigate the crash on their own out of a conviction—or at least a suspicion—that the facts had been incorrectly interpreted. They have now produced what they claim are both new evidence and new interpretations. As a result of their efforts, Mr. Gilman is demanding that the school board reconsider its dismissal of him. However, because the issues in this case extend beyond the question of his dismissal into the area of automotive safety, it has been decided that the matter will be placed in the hands of this, the Highway Safety Board of the State Motor Vehicle Bureau.

"For those of you who are uncertain about the nature of these proceedings," Mr. Eggleston continued, "let me explain that ours is an administrative commission. Our jurisdiction is to determine if there are grounds here for a full inquiry and formal administrative procedure. We are entitled to do this whenever there appears to be a pattern of automotive accidents that might require formal investigation. Since our inquiry is informal, we are able to dispense with some of the stricter procedures that usually go with full investigations. We are empowered only to report our findings to the State Motor Vehicle Bureau. The bureau may then take whatever action is called for, if any."

He reached under his desk and placed a pile of reports on it. He began passing them out, explaining, "We have had the minutes of the school-board hearing printed up. If you'll take a moment to look them over, we can do away with a lot of repetitious testimony today. I do want to remind you, though, that this hearing will differ a good deal from the school-board hearing. That dealt with the question of Mr. Gilman's dismissal, whereas we are inquiring into the question of whether a dangerous automotive condition exists."

There were several minutes of rustling as the men and women around the table examined the document. When the noise had subsided, Mr. Eggleston said, "I suppose the best way to start the proceedings would be to turn them over to Mrs. Carter, who is representing Mr. Gilman and the students and who will present their evidence and testimony. Mrs. Carter?"

Lydia stood and smiled at the gathering. Her eyes drifted from face to face as she tried to assess the attitude of each person present. She wanted to know who was sympathetic, who hostile, and who undecided. There was little point in addressing herself to the sympathetic ones—Mr. Case, Sam, Mr. Cassiday, and the kids—or to the hostile ones—Mrs. Parsons and the men from Federal Motors and their lawyers. They had pretty much made up their minds and probably couldn't be influenced. It was the others who had to be convinced: Mr. Twilly and the other members of the school board, and of course the three members of the safety board. As she spoke she made certain to direct her remarks to them.

"Ladies and gentlemen," she began in a level, well-modulated voice, "I am going to begin my presentation with an admission that may very well destroy our case before it even gets off the ground." Her approach was so unexpected that every person in the room looked startled. "I want to tell you candidly that I am by no means certain that the evidence and testimony I wish to present here are adequate." She paused to allow them to absorb this remarkable revelation.

"Does that mean that I am wasting your time?" Lydia continued. "Does that mean that this hearing is being held under false pretenses? My answer to that is a very strong No. Although this is not a court of law, I believe there is one courtroom principle which must be applied to this case, namely, the principle of reasonable doubt. For, while I am certain I cannot overwhelm you with proof that the brakes of Sam Gilman's bus were defective, I am satisfied that I can plant a reasonable doubt in your minds about the safety of those brakes. And if I succeed in doing that, I am certain that you will undertake a full-scale investigation not just of the brakes on Sam's bus, but of those on all the late-model buses produced by Federal Motors.

"I'm sure it has been apparent to all of you from the outset," Lydia went on, "that our main purpose in demanding these hearings has never been merely to get Sam's job back for him. Naturally, that is desirable, but our first concern— Sam's included—is to get people in authority to try to verify Sam's claim. Therefore if, when I'm finished presenting our case, you feel only that we *might* have something here, you will still have a duty to follow it up with an investigation."

Lydia scanned the faces around the table and felt she had won the first important battle. They were nodding their heads as if to say, "That makes a lot of sense." By confessing that her case was not as strong as it could be, she had managed to disarm their criticism. It would be harder for them to tell her they doubted her case when she freely admitted she doubted it herself.

"Before we get into the technical aspects of this dispute, I would like to take up the very critical matter of Sam's mental and emotional condition leading up to the accident. I'm afraid we have done a great disservice to Sam in accepting without critical evaluation the claim that he was disturbed for several months prior to the crash, and that he was actually in the care of a psychiatrist." Lydia noted that Mrs. Parsons was frowning and about to say something. Lydia smiled at her, quickly defusing the woman's explosion by smothering it with graciousness. "I can't blame anyone for believing it. There is an element of truth in it, and in the climate of indignation that surrounded the accident, it was easy to accept that explanation."

Mrs. Parsons closed her lips but still gazed dubiously at Lydia as if to say, "This had better be good."

"The contention that Sam was 'unstable' was especially convincing because Sam did nothing to combat it when it was raised at the school-board hearing. The reason why he did not should become clear to you when you learn what had been disturbing Sam during that time. I would like to call on him now to tell you about it."

Lydia nodded to Sam and sat down. Sam rose and hesitated for several moments, searching for a way to begin. Then slowly and gropingly, but with impressive dignity, he told them about his painful marriage, the attempt to save it by consulting with a marriage counselor, and the ultimate divorce. As he spoke Lydia kept her eye on Mrs. Parsons and observed a subtle change come over her features. The woman's eyes lowered and her lips puckered reflectively. She was too proud to admit she had acted with foolish haste, but her face admitted it for her.

Sam concluded and took his seat. Lydia remained seated, allowing the panel to react to his story. The mood in the air, she judged, was one of shame. No one was looking at anyone else, as if all were fearful of being blamed for condemning a man falsely.

Lydia now got to her feet and produced from her brief case the document which would nail this part of the case down. "I would like to read you a statement I secured from John P. Teague, the psychologist and marriage counselor referred to by Sam. 'Dear Mrs. Carter: I'm sorry I won't be in town to appear at the hearing, but this letter will confirm our telephone conversation in which I told you that Sam and Martha Gilman visited me once a week for some eleven months prior to their divorce in an effort to resolve their marital differences. Unfortunately, they were unable to reconcile those differences and were legally divorced early this year. Of course, it would be improper for me to comment on which of the two was more responsible for the failure. Indeed, the question itself makes little sense in the field of marriage counseling, for, just as it takes two to make a successful marriage, it takes two to make an unsuccessful one. But I will say that Sam made strenuous efforts to hold the marriage together. As for the question of his mental and emotional state, I can only give the opinion, as an experienced psychologist, that he did not display any evidence of a morbid or unstable psychological condition.' "

Lydia handed the letter to Mr. Case and asked him to pass it around. While this was being done Lydia said, "At the time Sam testified before the school board, he was still in a state of physical and mental shock from the accident. His divorce—the dissolution of a relationship of twenty-five years' standing—was still fresh in his mind. And so when the charge of emotional instability was brought against him at the hearing, he was too stunned and weak to deal with it. Rather than defend himself, as he has done today, he allowed himself to be defeated. His silence only served to strengthen the conviction that he was disturbed at the time of the accident."

Convinced that she had won the point, Lydia immediately plunged into the next and most important one. She knew that there is momentum in a case, and she wanted to take up the technical aspect while the members of the panel were still favorably disposed toward her.

"The problem on which we are all at odds is that of brake failure. Sam Gilman has claimed, and is prepared to swear under oath, that his brakes did not respond when he stepped on them coming down Temple Avenue. Mr. Case, on the other hand, tested the bus after the accident for brake failure but they worked perfectly under a wide variety of conditions. In light of this, our natural inclination is to doubt Sam's word. However, these three youngsters, who have known Sam for a long time, could not believe that he would lie. They raised a question which had not occurred to anyone else, namely, Might it not be possible for the brakes to fail on one occasion and work perfectly again thereafter? Admittedly, it is difficult for us to conceive of such a thing. Our sense of logic tells us that machines either work or don't work but can't do both at the same time. In spite of that logic, however, the children undertook a study of the brake structure of the bus in the hope of discovering some flaw which had eluded Federal Motors engineers."

A number of panelists smiled and murmured to one another. "I'm sure you're all thinking how presumptuous it was for children with no professional training to think they could find a defect in a system created by some of the best engineering minds in the country. Yet all of us can think of instances where even superbly engineered products failed because those who built them neglected to consider all the possibilities. In any event, I can only ask you to keep an open mind as Vernon Stevenson describes the conclusions he reached after intensively studying the brake structure of the type of bus Sam Gilman was driving. Vernon?"

Vernon, looking very scholarly, undid the string on a large manila envelope and drew out a number of sketches and papers. He then proceeded to explain the mental process by which he had arrived at his conclusions. At the beginning his voice cracked, but as he went on his presentation gathered force. When Vernon related how the strange behavior of the sink stopper in his hospital room had given him an important clue to the possible on-again–off-again behavior of the brakes, several people at the table, including Dr. Cordell, the safety board's engineer, looked at him with respect.

Finishing his analysis, Vernon passed his sketches and figures around the table and waited for questions. The four men from Federal Motors pored over the documents, conferred in low tones among themselves, and then Mr. Austin smiled. It was not a smile Vernon cared for. It was patronizing, as if the man were saying, "You're a very smart boy, but as you're not an adult we're not really obliged to take you seriously." Vernon felt his face grow warm as Mr. Austin said, "Tell me, Vernon, have you figured out what the odds are that the brake system would fail?"

"No," he replied guardedly. "I don't think you can quote odds because we still don't know what combination of conditions would have to occur to cause the failure. I suppose I'd have to say the combination was a rare one—but not an impossible one."

"And have you tested an actual brake system?"

"No, sir, I haven't."

"Well then," Austin said smoothly, "what we have here, ladies and gentlemen, seems to be little more than a theory. And with all due respect to this young man's excellent grasp of engineering principles, I have to remind you that he lacks even the rudiments of formal engineering training. It would not be difficult for any layman to look superficially at a technical design and say that under a rare combination of conditions, certain components might fail. But an engineer must go much farther than that, and I would venture to say that no qualified engineer . . ."

"I beg to differ," Mr. Case said, jumping to his feet. "I am a qualified engineer and I find more than a little merit in Vernon's explanation."

"We are not talking about merit," Mr. Austin replied calmly. "We are talking about proof. And as long as we are, I would like to offer this panel a report prepared recently by Federal Motors after putting a number of its late-model school buses through a variety of tests." He reached down and brought up a thick document bound handsomely in blue vinyl. "As it is rather extensive and we did not have time to print up extra copies for all of you to read at once, I will summarize it for you in a mere sentence or two. It says in effect that after rigorous testing under all sorts of conditions, our engineers were unable to produce a single example of failure. You're welcome, Mr. Eggleston, to look the report over at your leisure." Austin gave a confident smile and took his seat.

Suddenly Mr. Cassiday rose to his feet. "When you do look that report over, Mr. Eggleston, I hope you'll keep a number of things in mind, because I was involved in some of those tests and I'm by no means satisfied that we exhausted the possibilities."

The other Federal Motors men flashed warning signals at the young engineer, signals that told him that if he didn't keep quiet and sit down he might not have a job when he returned to the office.

Mr. Eggleston said, "Mr. Cassiday, you're not suggesting that Federal Motors has deliberately concealed or altered the results of its tests, I trust."

"No, sir, nothing like that. But since these two youngsters, David and Penny Case, visited our headquarters shortly after the accident, I have been working on some theories of my own. Vernon Stevenson may not be an experienced engineer, but I am, and I'm convinced that the brake failure could occur precisely the way he has described it. Furthermore, I am convinced that a great deal more testing remains to be done on this new type of brake system before it can be declared safe beyond a reasonable doubt. There are a number of atmospheric, speed, and other conditions that must be tried. I have prepared a kind of dissenting opinion suggesting areas in which the Federal Motors tests were insufficient. I begged Mr. Austin to present it side-by-side with his own, but he refused. So . . . I'm doing this on my own."

As the other Federal Motors men frowned, Mr. Eggleston accepted the document and placed it underneath the other. Then he said, "Mr. Cassiday, this is all well and good, but so far we have heard little besides theory. Can you, or anyone else here, provide hard factual evidence that Sam Gilman's brakes failed? Can anyone here demonstrate with concrete facts how, after such a failure, the brakes might work again?"

Lydia rose, her face clouded by concern. The chairman had uttered the very objection she had worried about all week long. Whether Mr. Eggleston was preparing to dismiss Sam's claim on those grounds, she did not know, but she did know her case would be in serious trouble if she didn't come up with a convincing argument.

She did have an argument left, but was it convincing? It was hard to say, but she had no choice other than to try it. "Mr. Eggleston, in the course of our research we came across an item which we consider to be of the highest importance. It's a clipping from the *Verona Ledger* with the headline, 'School Bus Mishap Injures Six.'" Lydia read the article about the school bus carrying thirty-two children that had struck a car stopped at a red light.

"We have spoken to the driver, Clifford Morgan, and to the Verona school board. It appears that the circumstances of that accident are amazingly similar to Sam's. The driver claimed that the brakes of his bus, a late-model Federal Motors vehicle, failed. The bus was tested and the brakes worked perfectly. They didn't believe Morgan either: he was fired."

"In other words," Mr. Austin broke in, "there is no proof

that Morgan wasn't negligent. Like Sam Gilman, he might have been using this brake failure business to excuse his recklessness."

Lydia felt anger rising. "Now just a minute, Mr. Austin . . ."

"I'm sorry, Mrs. Carter, but I'm growing weary of having the integrity of our company maligned today. As Mr. Eggleston just mentioned, we haven't heard one single fact, only theories and guesses and notions. Unless you can demonstrate otherwise, the similarity of the accidents here and in Verona must be considered pure coincidence. And as for the drivers' claims that the brakes failed—well, I must say frankly I find you a bit naive, Mrs. Carter. I'm sure many drivers would make up a story like that to keep from being fired. In fact, in all my years, I've rarely met a driver involved in any accident who admitted it was his fault. Forgive me for speaking so bluntly, but the reputation of my company is at stake, and millions of dollars worth of business may be lost if the public is allowed to believe even a shred of the story you have told us here today." He turned to the three members of the safety board and said, "I can only hope you will see this matter as we do."

Mr. Eggleston did not reply to him. Instead he said to the rest of the panel, "The board will recess for lunch. During that time we will review the arguments and evidence presented here. We will reconvene in this room in two hours, at which time we hope to have reached a decision."

Penny, David, and Vernon looked at Lydia for a quick indication of how the hearing had gone.

Her eyes were bleak and discouraged.

17
Turnabout

The meeting broke into little groups. The safety board remained behind. The Federal Motors men, with the exception of Mr. Cassiday, marched off. The school-board members lingered for several minutes in the corridor to discuss the case. Mr. Case spoke to his children for a minute, then joined the rest of the school board when it at last moved toward the elevators. That left Penny, David, Vernon, Lydia, Sam, and Mr. Cassiday. Mr. Cassiday broke off too, saying with a humorless laugh, "I think I'll spend lunch hour looking for another job."

Lydia and her entourage took the elevator to the main floor and decided to dine on hot dogs and cold drinks sold by the vendors in the little park across the street. They loaded up on them, found a bench, and ate in glum silence, their faces a depressing contrast to the springtime color around them. Vernon looked especially weary and discouraged, and rubbed his leg above the cast. "Darn!" he said, "I was counting on one person to come through."

"Who?" asked Penny.

"It doesn't matter now," he said, and everyone was so downcast they didn't bother to pursue his reference.

They lapsed again into silence, broken only by one question from Sam. "Lydia, how come you didn't tell the safety board about the visit those Federal Motors fellows paid me? Don't you think it would show them for what they are?"

"It might, but I'm certain Austin and Marley, if they admitted they visited you at all, would merely say they did it to stop a false story. You might end up looking like a man so desperate to get his job back that he'd make up any fantastic story. As Austin said, there are millions of dollars riding on this case, and the game gets rough when the stakes are that high."

"Then you think . . . ?"

"I think we've had it," Lydia said, and that was the last word spoken before they returned to the meeting.

The faces on each side of the table reflected the shift in the balance of victory and defeat as they took their seats after lunch. The Federal Motors men radiated confidence, Lydia and the children despair.

Mr. Eggleston called the meeting to order and immediately launched into his statement. "The State Highway Safety Board has reviewed the documents and testimony given this morning in the matter of Sam Gilman's petition to be rehired by the Aubrey Park school board. The case has not been an easy one to judge, for we have had to weigh a number of profoundly important factors. On the one hand, Federal Motors is faced with a serious blow to its prestige and financial standing; on the other, the lives and limbs of countless schoolchildren may be endangered. Naturally, our first responsibility is to the children, and we were prepared to give them the benefit of the doubt if we found any merit whatsoever in Mr. Gilman's claim."

Lydia shook her head. Mr. Eggleston had all but stated that the board found Sam's claim invalid.

"We wish to commend the industrious and public-spirited young people who labored so hard to demonstrate the truth of that claim. In a time of widespread public apathy, their involvement stands out as an example for all of us to follow. However, I regret to say that in this instance, their dedication is not enough."

Mr. Eggleston went on. "The representatives of Federal Motors have insisted that there is no factual evidence to support the claim of brake failure, and that the theory proposed by Vernon Stevenson has no correspondence to engineering reality. Although Mr. Stevenson's theory is supported by one of Federal Motors' own engineers, Mr. Cassiday himself admits that it is only theory. On the other hand, Federal Motors has not been content with theory, but has actually tested its bus brakes under a variety of conditions. And in spite of Mr. Cassiday's protest that the tests were not extensive enough, we are satisfied that Federal Motors has been conscientious in investigating Sam Gilman's claim. We therefore find that . . ."

Suddenly there was a commotion in the hall. The door opened and a black face poked tentatively inside. The face belonged to a middle-aged man with a perplexed, yet jolly expression. "Excuse me. Is this the Gilman hearing?"

"Yes," said Mr. Eggleston.

"That blasted secretary told me room 316, not 216. I tell you, the confusion in this place is unbelievable!" He was panting and perspiring profusely.

"Do you have business with this hearing?" Mr. Eggleston asked.

The man stepped into the room, patting his brow with a handkerchief. "I sure do. My name is Andrew Poole."

Vernon sat up straight in his chair. "Mr. Poole!"

"Ah, you must be Vernon," he said, waving a manila envelope in the air.

"Say, just what's the meaning of this?" said Mr. Austin testily.

Mr. Poole looked at Austin good-naturedly. "From the way you say that, I'll bet you're a Federal Motors man."

Mr. Eggleston asserted his authority. "Mr. Poole, we have just about concluded this hearing. If you have something to contribute, please identify yourself and state your business."

"Sure, sure. My title is Assistant to the Coordinator of Safety Programs of the State Motor Vehicle Bureau."

A look of recognition came into Mr. Eggleston's eyes. "You must be Bill Jordan's assistant."

"Right. Now as for my business, a few weeks ago this young man here, Vernon Stevenson, called me and asked if I'd help him run down some information on a couple of school buses that had been involved in accidents, one in Aubrey Park, the other in Verona. I had to go out of town for a week, and when I came back I had a big backlog of work to dig out of—you

know how it is. Anyway, I've only been able to get to the task in the last couple of days."

"What kind of information were you seeking?" Mr. Eggleston asked.

"The lot numbers of the brakes involved."

"And you've found them?"

"Yes, sir. The number on the Aubrey Park bus brakes was C-1456-L."

"And on the Verona bus?"

Mr. Poole smiled. "C-1456-L. Both brakes came from the same lot."

The members of the panel stirred, but Mr. Austin reacted quickly. "Mr. Eggleston, I don't believe that makes a bit of difference. There are thousands of Federal Motors buses on the road, and the fact that two involved in accidents had the same model brakes means nothing."

"Although I can't speak for the two other safety board members," said Mr. Eggleston, "I'm inclined to agree with Mr. Austin."

"Yes." Mr. Poole smiled. "But he said two accidents. I'm saying—six."

"Six!" Mr. Eggleston gasped. The meeting erupted into a hubbub.

Mr. Poole drew a piece of paper out of his file and read it aloud. "Evanston, Illinois—school bus rams car. Driver and seven children injured. Driver claims brakes failed. Manufacturer, Federal Motors. Brake lot number: C-1456-L. East Orange, New Jersey—school bus runs a stop sign. No one injured. Driver claims brakes failed. Manufacturer, Federal Motors. Brake lot number: C-1456-L. Tampa, Florida— school bus bumps school bus. Driver, one child injured.

Driver claims brakes failed. Manufacturer, Federal Motors. Brake lot number: C-1456-L. Columbus, Ohio—school bus coming to halt rolls onto railroad tracks. Bus evacuated and driven off tracks moments before train arrives. Driver claims brakes failed. Manufacturer, Federal Motors. Brake lot number: C-1456-L." Mr. Poole looked up. "Those four, plus Aubrey Park and Verona. Six accidents, six claims of brake failure, six Federal Motors buses, six brake systems with the same lot number. Nobody killed—yet." He dropped the file on the table with a loud slap and said, "You mentioned that this hearing was all but concluded. May I know what decision you'd reached?"

Mr. Eggleston put his head together with Dr. Cordell's and Mrs. Dorn's. Then he announced, "We were on the verge of finding Sam Gilman's claim invalid. But in view of this extraordinary new information, we are obliged to reverse ourselves. We intend to recommend to the State Motor Vehicle Bureau, the Interstate Commerce Commission, and the board of directors of Federal Motors that they thoroughly investigate the questions raised here today. In the meantime, we trust that Federal Motors will halt production on all school buses using brake lot C-1456-L, and will recall all those now on the road until the defect has been located and remedied. This hearing is adjourned."

18
Everybody Smile!

"My goodness, you gobbled down your breakfast!" Mrs. Case said to her son and daughter.

"Yes, we're being picked up any second now," David said.

"Usually you let the bus wait," his mother said.

"This morning isn't usual," he replied.

"Did you see this morning's *Telegram?*" Mr. Case said, peering over the top of it.

"We certainly did," said Penny.

Mr. Case lowered the paper and gave his children his full attention. "I want to tell you how proud I am of both of you."

David and Penny looked abashed. "Heck, all we did was ... Wait a second. I hear them!"

"Hear who? Say, what *is* that racket?"

Mr. and Mrs. Case rushed to their front window. David and Penny grabbed their books and opened the front door as a caravan of cars led by a school bus turned into their block. Children with ribbons, pennants, and noisemakers had their heads stuck out of every window.

The bus pulled up to their house, the doors opened, and down stepped Sam Gilman, beaming from ear to ear. "Well, she's an older model, but her brakes work. Still, I'm driving real slow and keeping my hand over the emergency brake, just in case my brakes go 'negligent' on me," he said to David. Penny had run back into the house to get her camera. As she returned, Vernon negotiated his way down the stairs of the bus on his crutches. With typical cleverness, he had devised a harness somewhat resembling a saddlebag on each crutch to carry his books, thus relieving his hands of extra burdens. He mugged for the camera, then took the morning newspaper out of one of the bags. "Did you see it?"

"Of course we saw it," Penny said. "But hold it up anyway. I want to take a picture of you and David and Sam holding the paper up, with the bus behind you."

"We want you in the picture too," Sam protested to Penny.

Mr. Case emerged from the house. "I'll be glad to take the picture. Get in there, Penny."

Penny joined her brother, Vernon, and Sam, and put on her prettiest smile as her father focused the camera.

"Can you pick up the fine print?" Sam asked.

"No, but I can get the headline: 'FEDERAL MOTORS RECALLS 1,000 BUSES FOR BRAKE DEFECT.' Now everybody smile."

Everybody smiled, and Sam Gilman's grin was the broadest of all.

Irwin Touster

became interested in writing about the law for young people as the father of two questioning boys and the brother of a lawyer. The co-author of several adult books, Mr. Touster lives in New York City.

Richard Curtis

is the author of fifteen juvenile and adult books, among them *Perils of the Peaceful Atom* (with Elizabeth Hogan) and *The Case for Extinction* (Dial). He lives in New York City.

Richard Cuffari

has illustrated many juvenile books, including *The Perez Arson Mystery* and *Gregor Mendel* (Dial). He lives in Brooklyn, New York.